THE GHOST PAINTS A PORTRAIT

FOURSQUARE BOOKS

THE GHOST PAINTS A PORTRAIT

THE GHOST PAINTS A PORTRAIT

A Nell Bane Novel

Nancy Parsons

THE GHOST PAINTS A PORTRAIT
Nancy Parsons

Published by
The Cheshire Press
A Division of The Cheshire Group, Inc.
PO Box 2090
Andover, MA 01810
www.cheshirepress.com

ISBN: 978-0-9960210-5-0
Library of Congress Control Number: 2015936374

Printed in the United States of America

This is a work of fiction. Any resemblance to individuals or
occupations are purely coincidental. All trademarks used herein are for
identification only and are used without intent to infringe on the
owner's trademarks or other property rights.

Cover art by Don Doyle

Parsons, Nancy
The Ghost Paints a Portrait

THE GHOST PAINTS A PORTRAIT

For Donald

Also by Nancy Parsons

More From The Better Mousetrap
with Dick Amsterdam

Bald As A Bean: The Experience of Sudden Hair Loss

Abigail's Unicorn

Ye Canna Join In Oor Games
Memories of a Scottish-American Childhood

Brothers of War: The P.O.W. Experience
with James F. Arsenault

The Dog That Managed Hedge Funds

Two-Thirds of a Ghost
A Nell Bane Novel

The Ghost Works A Puzzle
A Nell Bane Novel

The Ghost Ties a Double Knot
A Nell Bane Novel

THE GHOST PAINTS A PORTRAIT

*He sees what he wants to see and not what he does not
want to see. He looks at the things he ought to look at
and neglects those that need not be looked at.*

J.D. Salinger
A Taoist Tale:
Raise High The Roof Beams, Carpenter

*I met a lady in the meads,
Full beautiful—a faery's child,
Her hair was long, her foot was light,
And her eyes were wild.
They cried—La Belle Dame sans Merci
Thee hath in thrall!*

John Keats

THE GHOST PAINTS A PORTRAIT

Chapter 1

The Fitzmaurices, Franklin and Ann, lived in one of Newburyport's many quirky—and enviable—houses. In their case, in an old place out Water Street that had been remodeled and remuddled, extended and opened-up a dozen times over the place's century-and-a-half. The house had good vibes, Nell Bane had always thought, and a good view. The ocean was right across the street and no building intruded with a too-tall chimney or a ramshackle shed. Nell enjoyed visiting. The house was comfortable.

Ann Fitzmaurice, a portrait painter, had built a respectable reputation on the North Shore. And that was saying something, in Nell's opinion, for artists were thick on the ground. They came from all over the country to paint the seacoast and marshes, to set up studio-shops and angle for hangings in local galleries and in the venerable North Shore Arts Association on Gloucester's Pirate's Lane.

Ann's studio was at one end of the Fitzmaurices' vast front room and at the opposite end from the kitchen. Two banks of long windows washed this dual-purpose room with incredible ocean light and offered inspiring views.

"Very convenient," Ann often said. "I can cook and paint without having one occupation interrupt the other."

Indeed, the large room often smelled of baking cookies or roasting lamb that blended agreeably with the scents of artist's turps and gesso. Nell, a dedicated and masterful soup maker, found the aromas of the Fitzmaurice house delectable. She inhaled deeply and expectantly as she came through the side door. But the kitchen today was cold and unused and Ann's apron was the painterly one, its ticking stripes smeared with streaks and dabs of lead white, Prussian blue, cerulean and rose madder.

"You could hang that apron in the Museum of Modern Art," Nell told her, "and claim it's a Jackson Pollack. I stopped in to get those notes from the historical commission meeting, but if you can't get them right now, I won't disturb."

Ann Fitzmaurice laid her brush down with a sigh.

"No, now's as good a time as any. This thing needs some drying time, and I could use a break, in fact. Got time for a cup of coffee?"

"If you're sure you can be interrupted. Yeah, I'd love a cup."

Nell moved to Ann's easel to peer at the work in progress. The canvas was large—large and long—and the three-quarters figure of a woman, rendered there in great, slashing strokes of vine charcoal, was nearly life-sized. While most of Ann's drawing seemed almost brutal, Nell could see that she had already painted parts of the face—particularly the eyes and eyebrows—with meticulous care. Nell studied the scrubbed-in brushwork where Ann had begun darkening the background to silhouette the figure and bring it forward from the pale sepia-toned canvas. She got a whiff of turpentine.

"Is this your client?"

"This is my *subject,*" Ann told her. "Ramona O'Hara. Stuart Hammer, her husband, is my client."

Ann moved to the kitchen and poured two mugs of coffee but Nell, mug in hand, strayed back to the studio part of the room, drawn inexorably by the woman's painted image.

"She looks exotic," Nell said.

Ann's answer was a shrug.

"Perhaps. I don't know her very well yet. She's been quiet. He husband has done ninety percent of the talking, and he's very excited about this portrait. Ramona seems just a passive component. 'Stand there' I say.' She does. 'Look over here,' I say. And she does. She's pleasant. She's cooperative. But I don't think her heart's in this. She doesn't seem especially interested. Stuart though, he can't wait to have this enormous painting of his wife. Told me has already prepared a spot where she'll hang."

Nell shook her head in wonder. She couldn't imagine how her friend could manage a commission as bold as this one. Where did one start? How did the artist capture a likeness and translate it to canvas? And such a huge canvas!

"Oh goodness!" exclaimed Ann. "There he is. He's early! Way early. He said he'd be here at two o'clock. What time is it?"

"Eleven."

As Nell watched through the window, the man made his way delicately over the granite stepping-stones that delivered the Fitzmaurices' visitors from the parking court in front of the garage to the side of their house. His head was down and he watched his feet, which was necessary to safely navigate the stones. He was a trim man, Nell noted, with graying hair a little longer than fashionable and brushed carefully back. He arrived, safe and beaming, at the side door.

"I'm early," he explained when Ann swung it open, "but I just couldn't wait to see the painting."

"Well, you are a bit early, but come in, come in."

Ann's pique of just moments earlier seemed to Nell to be camouflaged nicely.

"This is my friend Nell Bane," Ann said, making introductions. "She's a writer. And this is Stuart Hammer. His wife is the subject of the portrait you saw on the easel."

Hammer's smile hadn't dimmed a kilowatt and he was shifting from leg to leg like a small boy needing the bathroom. His eyes shifted toward the studio portion of the room. "May I see?"

Ann relented.

"Certainly, but I warn you it has a long way to go."

Hammer needed no second invitation. He stepped across the room, but in front of the easel, his smile died.

"It's brown."

"Yes," Ann agreed. "That's under-painting. We're still in the earliest oil sketch phases, Stuart. I'm still working to get the angles right. Ramona's expression, the angles, the light— those are all considerations that have to be taken into account before I get down the final stages."

"Oh."

Stuart Hammer continued to stare for several moments. Then he turned to Nell. "Isn't she beautiful?" he demanded.

To Nell, the woman taking shape on the canvas looked like nothing more than strokes and streaks of paint. Nell could tell nothing about Ramona O'Hara, but she was politic.

"She is indeed," Nell said warmly. "And what an exciting adventure you have set yourself upon."

Stuart Hammer's high voltage smile returned and he looked radiantly at Nell. He had a moustache, Nell saw now. So pale and so carefully trimmed as to be nearly invisible.

"I'll just run upstairs and rustle up those papers," Ann Fitzmaurice said. "Nell, perhaps you wouldn't mind entertaining Stuart for a few minutes?"

Ann raised her eyebrows, signaling for help and Nell quickly stepped in.

"Of course. May I offer you coffee, Stuart?"

But Stuart Hammer didn't care for coffee just now. He was content, apparently, to stand and look Nell over, rocking from his heels to the balls of his feet and back again as he studied her. Study wasn't exactly the word, Nell felt. Scrutinize was more accurate.

"So you are a writer," he said. "What sort of writing do you do?"

"I write things for money," Nell told him. It was her standard answer to this question and the bluntness of her answer often forestalled further probing. Or made the questioner laugh, accept the comment at face value then change the subject. But Stuart Hammer wasn't deterred. He probed on, wanting to know the kind of writing she did.

"Ghostwriting," she told him. "People have stories they want to tell, but they lack the means or the time or the ability to tell them. So they tell their stories to me, I write them and readers are none are the wiser."

Stuart Hammer did not comment. He simply continued to rock and regard her, beaming all the while. Nell began to feel slightly uncomfortable. She could hear Ann moving about upstairs, and Nell wished she'd find those papers and hurry back. She and Stuart Hammer regarded each other some more.

"Here we are!" Ann was back and waving a sheaf of papers over her head. "Finally found them under the bed. I was reading them before I fell asleep."

"Thanks," Nell said. "Listen, I'll leave you two to get on with your business. No, no, Ann, these papers were all I needed and I'll see my way out. Very nice to have met you Mr. Hammer."

"Stuart!" He gave a small involuntary jump toward her as he said this. "Please call me Stuart. Promise now."

Nell smiled her promise and made her escape.

Chapter 2

Ann Fitzmaurice called the next day.

"Nell, I hope I haven't done something terrible."

Ann's voice was full of apology. Nell waited, wondering what Ann could have done that was so awful.

"Stuart Hammer asked for your number, and I'm afraid I gave it to him."

"What's so terrible about that?"

"Well," Ann said, "I got the impression that he might want to hire you. To write."

"So? That's what I do," Nell said pragmatically. "And I can take care of myself, Ann. I should probably thank you for the reference."

"Oh, thank goodness!" Relief flooded Ann's voice and she changed the subject. "Did you have a chance to look over those historical papers?"

And Ann and Nell moved to the subject of the local historical commission, upon which they were both serving a season. Or a sentence, as Nell sometimes put it. But as they chatted, a part of Nell's mind was wondering what Stuart Hammer could possibly want with her.

She found out shortly. Stuart Hammer lost no time calling.

"Mrs. Bane?" He was charming and urbane and his voice sounded deeper than Nell remembered. "Stuart Hammer. We met at Mrs. Fitzmaurice's. I hope you remember."

"Certainly I do, Mr. Hammer."

Nell chose not to gush or to natter platitudes. She simply let the silence between them broaden. This seemed to disconcert Hammer. His voice was slightly higher when he resumed speaking.

"I'll come to the point. Ann Fitzmaurice had said you were a writer...well, are a writer. Are. And I have a project in mind that I'd like to propose to you."

"Certainly," Nell said and waited some more.

When nothing was forthcoming on the other end of the line, she prompted him.

"Well? Go on."

"Oh. Well, as you know, Ann Fitzmaurice is painting a portrait of my wife, Ramona O'Hara, and after I met you I began to think how splendid it would be to have another sort of portrait—sort of a sister to the oil painting. This would be a portrait in words. I would like to hire you to write Ramona's story. She has a fascinating story, Mrs. Bane. Ramona has led a very interesting life. A fairy tale life. Yes, that's it. She's like a princess in a fairy tale. Could you do that, Mrs. Bane? Write her life story?"

Nell cleared her throat. She felt it had been quite a while since she'd spoken.

"Your proposal is something we certainly should explore, Mr. Hammer ..."

"Stuart," he interrupted. "Remember? I asked you to call me Stuart and you promised!"

"Ah. Ah, yes, I did. Well, *Stuart*, we could certainly discuss this. I'd want to explain to you how I work as well as how I am compensated. Also, I'd need to know more about your project. Then, if we are mutually satisfied with the results of our discussion, then yes, we could probably begin to work on your wife's story."

Stuart Hammer was delighted. This news, he assured Nell, was splendid. Just splendid. Now how were they to go about this exploration? And he hoped they could begin very soon.

Nell reflected, after hanging up the phone, that the gods of writers must be very good at traffic control for she rarely—in fact had she ever?—found herself with more commissions than she could handle at one time. And the fallow periods that inevitably came, were never so protracted that she couldn't pay her bills or buy ingredients to make soup. And as it happened Stuart Hammer's call had come in a fallow period. Nell would welcome the work, and she began to look forward to the meeting they'd arranged to have in Hammer's office the following week.

Chapter 3

"What are you doing with that chicken carcass?"

"What?" Nell's neighbor, Bunty Whitney, looked down in surprise at the remains of the deli chicken she'd been wrapping. "I'm preparing to toss it in the bin. Why?"

"May I have it?"

Now Bunty transferred her surprised look to Nell.

"What the hell for?" she asked. "I picked all the meat off the bones last night. Most of it anyway. There isn't enough chicken here to satisfy a cat."

Nell grinned.

"I don't want the meat. I want the bones. I'll make chicken carcass soup. You can roast a chicken, of course, and use the carcass, but a chicken from the deli is even better because it's easier. Did you save any juices from the bottom of the plastic dish?"

Wordlessly, Bunty indicated the plastic pan that the chicken had arrived in.

"Thanks!" Nell was delighted.

"You're getting stranger and stranger, did you know that?" Bunty said.

Nell laughed.

"Tactless of you to notice but probably true. You want to hear about my latest adventure?"

Now Bunty was all attention.

"Is the pope Argentinian? Of course I want to hear. Shall I brew some coffee or would you rather have wine?"

"What time is it?" Nell asked, peering at Bunty's kitchen clock. "Four o'clock. A little early for wine but so late in the day that coffee might keep me awake tonight. Wine it is."

"It's five o'clock somewhere," Bunty told her. "Hand me that corkscrew and start telling."

"The story starts with Ann Fitzmaurice," Nell began. "Ann accepted a commission from a man named Stuart Hammer to paint a portrait of his wife. A very large portrait. Practically life-size and three-quarter length. It's from the knees up, I mean."

Bunty nodded. She knew Ann Fitzmaurice, of course— and Franklin too—and was very fond of both of them.

"Go on," she prompted.

"I stopped by Ann's the other day to pick up some papers and while I was there, this man, Stuart Hammer, dropped in. Well, not dropped exactly. He had made an appointment with Ann, but he was about three hours early. Said he was so eager to see the portrait, he couldn't wait three more hours. I think Ann was sort of nettled. I mean the painting isn't ready to be viewed, and Ann explained it's far from finished—just barely begun in fact. But no, he had to see it."

Human beings fascinated Bunty Whitney. She had been a psychotherapist for most of her working life until she retired to devote her time to pottery, but while she claimed to be a reformed psychotherapist and vowed she was glad to be away from the "twiglets" who were her clients, she still grew avid with interest when the quirks and traits of the human race turned up.

"So that's background," Nell continued. "Apparently after I left, he winkled my phone number out of Ann. Stuart Hammer has decided he not only wants an oil portrait of his wife, he wants a word portrait too. That's what he's calling it—a word portrait. The whole enchilada."

"Okay," Bunty said neutrally, "so now what?"

"I'm meeting him at his office next Tuesday. At Talcott College. He teaches there."

"Talcott College for Women," Bunty said meditatively. "Somewhere on the North Shore, isn't it?"

"It is," Nell replied, "Only it isn't called 'for Women' anymore. They started admitting men a few years back when it became unfashionable—or illegal—to have same sex schools. So now its just Talcott College."

"How many men are enrolled there now?" asked Bunty. "Three? If I'm remembering correctly, Talcott used to be a very fancy—i.e. very expensive—college for young women who didn't have a great deal of intellectual promise but did have very wealthy parents looking for someplace credible to stash the girls between their coming out parties and their society weddings."

"Bunty!" Nell pretended to be shocked, but in truth, she had to admit Bunty was mostly right.

"Well, I can't imagine there'd be too many men who'd fit into the student body. Or who would want to," Bunty cheerfully defended her position.

"Probably not."

Nell shrugged, but Bunty changed the subject.

"Tell me about your soup. What are you going to do with my old, used chicken bones?"

So Nell told Bunty about chicken carcass soup and promised to save some for her.

CHICKEN CARCASS SOUP
1 leftover carcass from a roasted chicken
Pan juices saved from the roasted chicken
2 T butter
2 onions, coarsely chopped
3 carrots, peeled and coarsely chopped
10 whole cloves
1 inch fresh ginger root, peeled and finely chopped
Generous gratings of fresh nutmeg
2 T butter
 1 lb mushrooms, sliced
2 ribs of celery, chopped
Any leftover chicken cut from the carcass

In a large pot, Nell slowly cooked the onions and carrots in the butter. When the vegetables softened, she cracked the chicken carcass as much as possible and put the bones back in the pot, pushing them down before addeding cold water to just cover everything. The ginger, cloves and nutmeg were added next, and Nell brought the soup to the simmer, covered the pot and left it for one hour.

When the soup had cooled, Nell removed the bones and pulled off as much meat as possible. This, she set aside. She covered the soup with plastic wrap and chilled it overnight. The next day she skimmed the solid fat from the surface of the soup and heated it slowly. Meanwhile, she cooked the mushrooms in 2 T butter until they were golden brown and added these to the soup along with the chopped celery and leftover chicken. She simmered the soup until the vegetables were cooked softened, then adjusted the seasonings and served.

Chapter 4

Talcott College could have posed for a postcard captioned *Autumn in New England.* In fact, Nell was sure she'd seen photos of the campus on a couple of old calendars and in boutique card shops offering glossy prints glued onto heavy stock. On this Tuesday the sugar maples, wearing red and gold, had already littered the ground and stone walls with their brilliant leaves.

It was easy enough to enter the main gate (stone pillars, fancy iron arch) and to follow the gentle curve of road to the visitors' parking lot. Once afoot, though, Nell had to stop three different students to ask directions to Burton Hall before she was finally able to climb the stairs of the white-pillared brick building where she'd been told she would find the history department. Stuart Hammer's office was on the second floor and his door was open. Murmurs came from within and Nell, peering around the doorjamb, glimpsed Hammer at his desk in conversation with a student. He seemed to sense rather than see her and looked up with a quick smile.

"I'll be with you in a second, just as soon as I finish up with Miss Witledge."

And indeed, Miss Witledge, who looked awfully young to be a college student, came scurrying out directly, her shoulders rounded as if to protect the armload of books pressed against her chest. She glanced sideways at Nell and quickly averted her eyes.

Then Stuart Hammer was in the doorway, shaking Nell's hand and beaming as he had the day they'd met at Ann Fitzmaurice's.

"Come in, come in. Did you have any trouble finding the place?"

Nell assured him that she had not

Hammer gestured toward the chair recently occupied by Miss Witledge, and Nell, sitting down, felt she was taking a supplicant's position. Felt like a student bracing for a conference with a professor and perhaps expecting to beg for mercy on a grade. Hammer resumed his chair behind the desk and grinned at her. As she had at Ann's, Nell fell a little off balance.

"Well?" Hammer demanded pleasantly. "How do we begin?"

Now Nell was on more familiar territory. Her confidence returned.

"We begin with you telling me about your project," she said, "Tell me why you want to have this story written and who you want it written for. In other words, tell me what you want it to accomplish. And then I'll tell you how I work and how I am compensated."

Hammer nodded. "So I go first, yes?"

"That's the place to start."

He nodded again and, looking very pleased with himself, leaned back in his chair, making himself comfortable. Hammer placed his fingers together in a tent shape and tapped them as he organized his thoughts.

"My wife, Ramona O'Hara, is a very interesting woman," Stuart Hammer said. "A fascinating woman with a fascinating story, and that story deserves—indeed begs—to be told. Not only that, Ramona is a *beautiful* woman—well, you probably saw that in the portrait Mrs. Fitzmaurice is painting."

Nell, who had seen only the streaks of underpaint and the strokes of charcoal in Ann's preliminary oil sketch, had been able to see nothing of Ramona O'Hara's startling beauty, and she hardly knew how to respond to Hammer's claim. She decided to veer in a slightly different direction.

"Ann Fitzmaurice is a very talented portraitist and I am confident she will capture an excellent likeness of your wife."

Apparently the sidestep worked, for Stuart Hammer beamed at her again.

"So you are going to tell me Ramona's story," said Nell, picking up the conversation's original thread, "and I will write it. But tell me—why will you be narrating Ramona's story? Surely she would be the better one to tell it, wouldn't she?"

Stuart Hammer looked surprised.

"I can't really see why you'd need to speak with Ramona," he said. "I am looking forward to authoring her story. A sort of surprise for her, you see. A gift. But I can assure you, I know her story very well—intimately, I might say."

"So I won't have access to Ramona during this project?" she asked. "I'd just like to clarify that."

Nell was taken considerably aback. And she wondered just how she would handle this narrative wrinkle, but deciding not to prejudge it, she troweled over this odd detail for the time being.

"I will have to decide on the voice, of course" she said, thinking aloud. She frowned. "I'd prefer it to be first person but..."

Her frown deepened as she thought. Stuart Hammer watched her patiently. Finally Nell shrugged off her reservation.

"Well, we'll see how it works. Now let me tell you how I work, Stuart," she said. "I listen to my clients' stories, and I am always very interested in knowing what they hope to achieve with the written words. Who are they writing for? What is the purpose of the written piece. Now you have said you want a word portrait to stand as a companion piece to the oil portrait Ann is painting, have I got that right?"

Stuart Hammer quickly assured her that she did.

"I will record your narration on this little gizmo..." Nell held up her small digital recorder, "and at the same time, I'll make notes. I anticipate that it will probably take several sessions at the very least to collect all the information. It will depend on you and the amount of material you can provide. Then I will write a first draft which you will read and comment upon, indicating any errors or revisions you'd like to see made."

She looked at Stuart Hammer to gauge his reaction. He was leaning forward now and seemed to be following her avidly.

"Okay? Very well. I will estimate the number of hours this project will probably take and present that estimate. If you accept, I will require one third of the payment to begin work. When the project is about two-thirds complete—and I will establish when that is—the second payment will be due. The final third will be due upon delivery of the finished manuscript. We can speak at some point about publication options—I have an associate who can be of great help here—but publishing costs, whatever they turn out to be, will be additional and quite apart from the writing."

Stuart Hammer was nodding enthusiastically.

"Yes, yes. I accept. I certainly accept. Shall we begin?"

His alacrity startled Nell. She hadn't expected to begin

instantly.

"Best if you let me write up a contract," she said. "Just an informal one, but I'd also like to collect my things and be ready to get to the hard work. However we can arrange a time for our first session, if you'd like."

Stuart Hammer flipped open his Daytimer and Nell brought up the calendar on her cell phone and together they set a time to begin Ramona O'Hara's story.

Chapter 5

Indian summer and Nell had a case of reverse spring fever.

"Is that possible, Robert?" she asked as they crossed Beacon Street and entered the Public Garden.

Her old friend, Robert Hutchins, chuckled.

"Anything's possible, I guess. I've never heard of reverse spring fever, but I can certainly understand how it could overtake you."

"The air is redolent of autumn leaves," Nell rhapsodized, "and all above us arches October's bright blue weather. In another month," she instructed Robert, "November's skies will be that roiling navy blue-gray and we'll be planning for Thanksgiving and that will be nice too. Where shall we have lunch?"

At Nell's insistence they had stopped into DeLuca's Market and ordered sandwiches to eat in the park, and now Nell marched to the edge of the lagoon and claimed a vacant bench. Robert joined her. Nell partially unwrapped a sandwich and peeked in.

"This one's yours," she told Robert. "Capicola. Very brave of you."

They'd both ordered cracked pepper turkey and Swiss on sourdough, but at the last minute Robert had added capicola to his sandwich order. Nell had shuddered.

"What exactly is that anyway, capicola?"

"It's dry-cured Italian ham. Very hot. Jerry taught me about it. Not to your taste at all."

"How is Jerry?" Nell asked. Jerry Gasso, Robert's partner, was a great favorite of Nell's. He was lively and funny and an on-going source of energy and mischief. She tweaked a fragment of turkey out of her sandwich and nibbled it out of her fingers.

"Excellent," Robert said, answering her question. "Splendid in fact. He has started a new commission. A politician has moved into a house on the Hill, on Louisburg Square in fact, and he and his wife have gutted all four floors. The wife has hired Jerry to handle the interior design, and he's up to his eyebrows in fabric swatches and paint chips. Talks of little else. You probably won't see him again for six months and meanwhile *our* whole place is draped in velvets and linens. I only hope I can hold out."

Robert bit into his sandwich, chewed and swallowed.

"So you're about to start work again," he told her, changing the subject. "A reference from Ann Fitzmaurice, I understand."

"Um-mmm. A portrait of Ramona. Ann's doing the oil paint version and I am going to create a word portrait. I'm not exactly clear how I'm going to do that."

"What is Ramona like?" Robert answered.

"I have no idea yet," Nell said. "Very beautiful, I'm told. The possessor of a *fas*-cinating story—according to her husband. Beyond that I'm in the dark. I know more about her husband actually."

"And?"

As Nell's dear friend and sometime agent, Robert Hutchins was always interested and supportive.

"Stuart Hammer is a professor of ancient history at Talcott College. He's a small man—very dapper in a rather old-fashioned way. Somewhere in his early sixties, I'd guess, and I'm assuming Ramona is younger. It was hard to tell anything about her from the beginnings on Ann's easel. Stuart lights up like a night game at Fenway when he says her name. Kind of romantic, really."

They sat in companionable silence, gazing across the sleepy water toward the Lagoon Bridge. Willow branches trailed on the pond's surface like a woman's lank hair. The sun that had pulsated with heat all summer long, now felt loving and lazy, and Robert and Nell were in no hurry to leave.

"Oh!" Nell suddenly had a thought. "You might get involved in this project too, Robert. Stuart Hammer will probably need help publishing his wife's story. I'll keep you in the loop."

"A portrait of Ramona," Robert Hutchins mused. "Could be very interesting. Interesting indeed."

Chapter 6

"Before you start telling Ramona's story," Nell said, "Perhaps you could provide some background—some things about yourself, how you met Ramona, things like that."

Stuart Hammer looked surprised, then disappointed. He stared at her for a few moments, but Nell held her ground and never lost her smile as she held it.

"Oh," said Stuart Hammer. "Well, yes, I see. Of course."

But he looked uneasy.

"Perhaps we could cover that background stuff rather casually," Nell suggested. "Is there someplace we can sit down over a cup of coffee?"

And so Stuart Hammer had escorted her across the Talcott campus to the student union where he seated her with courtly ceremony at a formica table and hustled away to fetch two cups of coffee from a machine at the end of the cafeteria line.

"We have a coffee maker in the history department," he told her as he delivered the paper cup of coffee and a wad of paper napkins, "but it is ghastly stuff. The first person to arrive in the morning makes a big pot and it sits there on the burner all day, growing more bitter and syrupy by the hour."

Nell shuddered.

"Then I am very grateful for the invitation to the student union," she told him. "It is also a way for me to see more of the campus. It is quite lovely. Spectacular even."

Hammer, stirring his coffee, nodded.

"Have you been on the faculty here for a long time?"

He leaned back, considering.

"Yes," he concluded. "A long while."

Nell waited expectantly, but more details didn't come. This wasn't going terribly well. Stuart Hammer was going to have to be more forthcoming—present more fully developed answers and information—if they were to succeed at drawing their portrait of Ramona.

"Professor of history—ancient history," she said prompted encouragingly.

"Correct."

"Do you like teaching?" she asked desperately.

"I do. Yes."

Another silence ensued. Nell decided to shift the approach.

"I believe Ann said you live in Ipswich, Stuart. Tell me—is that your home town?"

"No," Stuart Hammer said carefully, "I grew up in Belmont. That's outside of Boston, you know."

Nell nodded and murmured that she did know, and waited for Hammer to pull further on this thread.

"Brothers and sisters?" she prodded.

"No. Oh no. Just me and my parents. I was an only child," he added unnecessarily.

"You went to college..." Nell said encouragingly. She felt like she was leading the witness.

"Indeed. I went to Bates. Up in Maine."

Nell nodded. "Yes. And then?"

"Then? Then I moved back home to Belmont. Continued my studies locally, earned my doctorate, and went job hunting. I was hired almost immediately by Talcott College as their professor of ancient history—that was years ago, of course—and the rest is history."

He chuckled.

"Not ancient history though."

His own little joke seemed to amuse him and he continued to smile at the joke's success.

Nell stretched the corners of her mouth encouragingly and waited some more.

"It was Talcott College for Women at the time," Hammer amplified.

Nell had applied her expression of spellbound listener. She hoped she had anyway.

"Fascinating," she told him. "Please go on."

"Well," said Stuart Hammer, thinking. "Then I met my wife. My first wife," he added quickly. "Minnie Poole. Minerva."

"Minnie Poole," repeated Nell. "What a wonderful name. Almost Dickensian. Was she a Talcott student?" Nell asked.

"Minnie? No. She was a librarian—the head librarian. And she was quite a few years older than I." He shook his head, apparently remembering.

"Minnie. She was something! Jolly. Had a great big laugh. The library was supposed to be hushed and silent, of course, but Minnie's laugh would just explode at the oddest times and ring out through the silence. Everyone would look up—startled—but the curious thing was, no one was annoyed. Minnie's laugh was just so infectious you had to smile. You had to join."

Stuart Hammer, remembering, smiled sadly.

Nell smiled too.

"That's lovely," she said. "A lovely image. Please tell me more.'

Stuart thought."

"Minnie was the heiress to the Has-Bean fortune."

"I beg your pardon?"

"Don't you remember Has-Beans? They were on almost every New England dinner table on Saturday nights. Minnie's grandfather, Arthur Poole, developed the family's old baked-bean recipe into a commercial product. He packaged it and sold it, but it was her father who turned the beans into a household name by aggressively marketing the product. He realized that housewives—oh, back about 1920 it was—that housewives were looking for convenience, and he short-cutted the traditional twenty-four-hour process of preparing baked beans for Saturday night suppers. 'Let *us* soak your beans!' was his slogan. And canned baked beans from Has-Beans became a pantry staple."

Nell had a flashback.

"I do remember!" she exclaimed delightedly. "I had three miniature cans of Has-Beans that I played with when I was a tiny child. I had this little pretend stove and I pretended to cook my Has-Beans on it."

The memory was a happy one, and for a few moments Nell was light-years back in her own past. Then she was brought up sharply, afraid she had thrown Stuart's narration badly off-track, but after a few moments, he took it up again.

"Well. Minnie's daddy—young Arthur they called him—brought home the bacon, and he brought it home in sizeable servings. Arthur the Elder had bought a big parcel of land in Ipswich, and Arthur the Younger built a house on it. House...well more of a mansion. Had stables in those days and fine horses. Big garages for the cars he collected. Minnie inherited the whole thing when her parents passed away."

"So you were married to the Has-Bean heiress," Nell summarized gently. And she smiled in case Stuart Hammer thought she was being flip, but he smiled too.

"Minnie had a little jingle," he admitted, "that she'd sing around the house. 'Make our beans *your* beans / Always ask for Has-Beans / Has-Beans! Has-Beans! / Rootie-toot-*toot!*'"

Nell pinched her lips and with some difficulty suppressed a laugh. But when Stuart Hammer offered a small, qualified smile, she allowed herself to laugh outright. Stuart joined her although his mirth seemed to Nell to be a little sad.

"What happened to Minnie?" she asked when her laughter quieted.

"She had an accident," he said quietly. "She fell down a flight of stairs and died of complications from her injury."

He shook his head at the thought and shifted onto one hip in order to pull a handkerchief from a side pocket. He wiped his nose efficiently and thoroughly. Nell looked away delicately. She peered into the depths of her coffee cup and thought about calling it a day, but she hadn't yet accomplished all she wanted to know.

"We haven't spoken yet of Ramona. When and how did she come into your picture?"

Hammer brightened a bit.

"Ramona. Ah. Well I was living in Ipswich..."

"... in the house built by the Has-Bean king?"

"Yes. I guess you could call me the heir to the Has-Bean fortune."

This second, weak pass at humor was somewhat out of character, Nell realized. She looked at him encouragingly.

"I was still teaching my classes at Talcott, of course, but the nights were long and they were lonely. And one evening I stopped into a bar."

He lowered his voice and leaned in a bit across the table

as he made this confession.

"A place called the Bowsprite down in Beverly. I'm not a drinking man exactly, but I wanted a little company. Wanted people around me for a change. A little noise, you know. Conversation. Maybe some music. Anyhow, I took a seat at the bar and ordered a glass of ale. And then she was there with the ale. Ramona. The most beautiful woman I'd ever seen. Dark. Sensational. I thought immediately of Helen of Troy. *Is this the face that launched a thousand ships?* I thought."

"*And topped the topless towers of Illium,*" Nell contributed.

"*Sweet Helen,*" said Stuart Hammer, taking up the verse, "*Make me immortal with a kiss.* Well, I went back to the Bowsprite the next evening. And the evening after that. And I worked up my courage and asked this beautiful woman her name. 'Ramona O'Hara' said she and on she went, wiping the bar, serving customers, chatting them up. And every time she paused to chat with some other man—to flirt with him a little— I felt a surge of jealousy. I'd never felt jealous before, but at that point jealousy seized me. Inflamed me. Ramona O'Hara was like a drug and I couldn't stay away from the Bowsprite."

At the end of this speech, Stuart sat back in his molded plastic chair, far away from Talcott College and its student union and far away from Nell Bane who sat opposite him.

Nell waited some more and finally tried priming the pump.

"And then you worked up the courage to ask her out?"

"Oh no!" Hammer said quickly. "Not right away, no. But every chance I got, I asked her about herself. She'd give me an answer. Just a crumb. Ramona, she said, when I asked her name. Then off she'd go to draw a draft for someone but the next time she came to my end of the bar, I'd ask another question. O'Hara, she said when I pressed her to know more. I asked her if she were Black Irish and she said yes. I have to confess I'd take these jewels of information away each night and they would feature in all my dreams. And the next night I'd be back at the Bowsprite for more. I couldn't get enough of Ramona O'Hara."

Hammer lapsed into reverie, and once again Nell waited.

"Stuart," she told him finally, breaking his spell, "I think we've accomplished what I hoped to get today. I wanted to know your background, but I think we should stop before you get any farther into your story about Ramona. I think we should save that for another session. But thank you for sharing something of your own background. It will help my writing to know a bit of background."

She peered into the dregs of her mostly-empty coffee cup. She stuffed her crumpled napkin into the cup and stood to go.

"There's one more issue we have to settle at the outset," Nell said. "You'll recall that our contract calls for one third of my compensation to be paid at the beginning of the project. I think we've begun, therefore..."

"Oh, most surely," Stuart Hammer said quickly.

He removed a checkbook from an inside pocket in his jacket and quickly wrote a check. He didn't have to ask or confirm the amount she'd named in the contract. That, Nell took as a positive sign. He handed the check over with a smile.

"I look forward to telling Ramona's story," he said. "Now. Let me walk you to your car."

"That would be lovely," she answered. "Very thoughtful.

And good as his word, Stuart Hammer escorted her to the parking lot and saw that she was securely bundled inside her Saab.

"Seatbelt fastened?" he asked, leaning in solicitously to inspect. "Ah. Good."

He closed her door carefully and waited while Nell backed out of her parking space. As she shifted into first gear and pointed the nose of her car toward the gates, he gave a salute of farewell. Nell acknowledged this with a little wave.

"Rootie-toot-*toot!*" she exclaimed, driving off. And she laughed.

Chapter 7

"What do I know now that I didn't know yesterday?" Nell asked herself.

She took an inventory.

She knew some things about Stuart Hammer. She knew he had been the only child of elderly parents and she surmised that he had been, as both man and boy, pampered and sheltered.

She knew he had gone away to college at Bates and returned home to his parents in Belmont while he earned a doctorate. She knew he had been hired to teach ancient history some years ago at Talcott College, and she reflected that he was neither adventurous nor restless, since he had remained at the first institution that had hired him.

She'd learned some interesting facts about his first wife, Minerva Poole, the heiress to the Has-Bean baked bean fortune, and she'd gathered that until she met Stuart Hammer, Minnie Poole had never been married. From Stuart's brief descriptions, she thought she'd like Minnie Poole very much.

She knew Minnie had died of complications following a fall down a set of stairs, and surmised it must have been a very violent fall indeed. She wondered what had caused the fall.

She reflected that Stuart Hammer seemed to miss Minnie very much.

She knew that Stuart's present wife, Ramona O'Hara, was to be the subject of her work, but so far her information about that subject was limited to Stuart's descriptions of her beauty and a few umber strokes of paint on Ann's easel.

Nell sighed.

"I have a lot to learn," she said out loud.

But she discovered she was looking forward to the lessons, the first one due to start the following week. In the meantime, she decided to try a very strange soup recipe she'd found called Dill Pickle Soup.

DILL PICKLE SOUP
5 T butter
5 medium carrots, shredded
2 large russet potatoes, cubed (about 2 cups)
3 large dill pickles, shredded
1 cup flour
1 cup sour cream
5 cups water

Combine water, butter, carrots and potatoes in a saucepan. Bring to boil and cook until potatoes are tender. Whisk together the flour and sour cream in a separate bowl. Add enough of the potato water to make a paste, then slowly, so as to avoid curdling, stir the paste into the soup stock to thicken. Bring soup just to a boil and remove the pan from the heat. Add the pickles and pickle juice to taste, then taste for the need for salt and pepper.

At the recipe's conclusion, Nell was warned not to add the

pickles until the very end of the recipe for an early addition would cause the potatoes to harden. How very curious Nell thought.

Chapter 8

It was raining when Nell, head down against the wind and cross-stepping to avoid puddles on the sidewalk, made her way across the Talcott campus. Ordinarily she liked rain, but this was a thoroughly aggravating rain—mean and wind-driven—that yanked the season's late leaves off branches and plastered them soddenly against everything they hit. Including Nell's legs. She grunted involuntarily as she splashed into a puddle, punctuating her grunt with an uttered "Damn!"

Nell stopped finally and looked up through the rain to get her bearings. She located Burton Hall ahead, lowered her head again, and splashed on.

So it was with wet soles and damp stockings that Nell took the student's chair in Stuart Hammer's office. Chilled and soggy, she decided even Burton Hall's bitter, warmed-over coffee would be welcome.

Stuart Hammer was beaming. He alternatively leaned back in his chair and lurched forward across the desk in his eagerness to begin.

"I'm ready," Nell declared at last. She had the digital recorder running on the desk within range of Stuart's voice and had her pen poised over a pad of paper just in case she had to make a note.

"Start wherever you wish Stuart, even if it is in the middle of the tale. I'm prepared to sort out the timeline when I write the first draft."

He was ready. Eager.

"Well, Ramona was born in Ireland," Stuart Hammer began. "Born in a tiny cottage—a fisherman's cottage—some ways west of Castlebar. To get to Castlebar," he explained to Nell in a kindly aside, "you'd travel northwest from Galway which is on Ireland's western coast. But then from Castlebar, you have to travel on to Carrowbeg then follow smaller and narrower roads beyond that till you'd come to the village of Carrach Duh. That's Irish for 'black bog', and the place hardly qualifies to be called a village, although it may qualify as a black bog."

He paused to look at Nell.

"Have you been to Ireland, Nell?"

"Just to Shannon," she told him. "A stopover at the airport on a trip so that hardly counts."

Hammer nodded and took up his tale.

"Well, Carrach Duh was little more than a pit stop—a few cottages strung out along the road with a simple grocer's and a pub to anchor the village. If you wanted to go to church or to school, you had to travel to the next, more prosperous village.

"The family mumbled along the poverty line—often dipping below the poverty line, if I'm any judge of what Ramona's told me, and rarely rising above it. Furthermore, the family was large. There were a number of children, a mother who was often sickly and a father who was not often there and when he was, he was usually drunk."

Hammer folded his hands and smiled happily.

"Now here is a romantic part of the story," he promised. "Ramona's mother was Black Irish. Do you know what that is, Nell?"

Nell nodded. "Spanish Armada ..."

"Exactly," Stuart Hammer was quick to wrest the narration away from her. "Yes. She—the mother—was descended from some sailor who'd been washed ashore when the great Spanish Armada was shipwrecked off Ireland's coast in 1533. Of the nearly one-hundred-thirty ships, twenty-four were smashed up on the rocks in a storm after the Armada's defeat at Gravelines. Those sailors who survived the wreck, left their mark on the population—a mark that survives even today when you see an Irishman with dark coloring or black hair. And it was tradition in the family that whenever a baby was born with that ancestor's dark, Spanish coloring, then the child was given a Spanish name. Ramona, like her mother, is Black Irish—a dramatic blending of Celtic and Spanish bloods. And so, attached to that great Irish surname O'Hara, is a Christian name straight out of Andalusia. Ramona."

He sat back in triumph and gazed at Nell. She shifted uncomfortably on the hard chair. She had certainly heard the Black Irish myth, and she was pretty sure it was just that— myth. And she thought that Stuart Hammer, as a professor of ancient history, should have been able to recognize the story as such. Perhaps his area of ancient history didn't extend as far north as Ireland though. Maybe it just covered Greece and Rome and Mesopotamia. Nell wasn't sure. She decided not to question Hammer on this however. Well. Let his story spin out, then she'd see.

"Life was hard." Stuart took up the tale again. "The father— O'Hara—was mean when he wasn't sober, and he was rarely sober. He abused his wife and his children, and Ramona took more than her share of abuse, for her sister Kath was sickly like the mother, and Ramona frequently had to step in between her father and her sister. To help with the family expenses, Ramona talked her way into a job at the village pub, first as a scullery maid, washing glasses and mopping up, but she soon worked her way up to serving at the bar, even though she was too young to be legally doing that work. Apparently Carrach Duh was too far for there to be much oversight of minors.

"Well, Ramona had an uncle. Uncle Padriac, she called him, and he was on her all the time. Teasing her, bullying her, lusting after her. And he was at Kath too until the poor girl could take it no longer and took her own life. And with that, Ramona, at age sixteen, had enough. She ran away—ran to Castlebar and when that wasn't far enough, she went to Galway. She easily got barmaid jobs along the way, but Padriac, that bastard, tracked her down each time. Finally she went to Dublin, figuring Ireland's biggest city would be big enough to allow her to disappear.

"Padriac didn't follow her to Dublin, but she was scouted by a fellow who was making a film. An art film. You see, Ramona was quick and talented as well as beautiful, and she knew how to be personable and friendly with her customers, while at the same time never over-stepping boundaries. And this casting director saw all this and appreciated it, and he cast her in a film.

"Wouldn't you know it? The film did well. Was what they call a sleeper. And it won all sorts of awards and accolades at those film festivals they hold on the Rivera and places like that. Well, someone saw the film and somehow word got back to Padriac O'Hara that little Ramona had become a movie star. At that point, even Dublin wasn't far enough. Ramona packed her kit and fled to Boston where her mother's sister Carmela agreed to take her in."

Here Stuart Hammer paused in his story and looked at Nell.

"I'm parched from talking," he told her. "Can I get you anything? Water? Tea?"

"Tea would be wonderful!"

Nell was eager to wrap her cold fingers around a warm cup of anything. She pulled her sweater more tightly around her as Hammer trotted off to get the beverages. Nell, looking around the office, suffered a flashback to her own college days and of sitting for conferences in fusty, cluttered faculty offices. Ill-lit. Untidy. This office didn't seem to match its natty little occupant who was so carefully turned out with bow ties and coordinated pocket handkerchiefs.

"Here we are!"

He was back and Nell reached out gratefully for the Styrofoam cup.

"Where was I? Oh. Boston and Aunt Carmela."

Stuart Hammer took up his thread without hesitation.

"Aunt Carmela lived in the projects in South Boston and there was hardly room in the flat for one more, but Ramona didn't care. She would have been grateful for a pallet on the floor at that point. And she wasted no time in looking for work and in landing a barmaid's job at a local pub, but she was determined to get out of South Boston, which wasn't to her taste, and to better herself and rise in the world."

This recitation was beginning to take on a Horatio Alger quality, Nell thought. Stuart Hammer's language was starting to smack of the nineteenth century, but maybe that was to be expected from a professor of ancient history.

"Southie wasn't that much different from Ireland," Stuart continued. "Or from Galway, for that matter, or from Castlebar or even from Carrach Duh. An Irish pub is a universal thing apparently.

"So Ramona was tending bar and eventually she started taking classes over at UMass Boston. Psychology and sociology—subjects in which she was already well experienced from her bartending and through the canniness developed in outwitting Padriac.

"And about this time you met Ramona?" Nell asked. She felt like she hadn't spoken in ages.

"Around this time, yes" he said, "or a bit after. Ramona had come up in the world and was living in a small apartment on the North Shore and working at a very nice place in Beverly—the Bowsprite. And I think I told you how I stopped in there one evening, quite by chance, and met her. Well, she enchanted me. I couldn't stay away. I am not a courageous man, but I was emboldened to ask her to dinner. I couldn't help myself. Then one thing led to another, and I worked up the courage to ask her to marry me. I think we were both surprised by the proposal and even more surprised by her acceptance. It all happened very quickly."

Stuart Hammer sat back in his chair, glowing with pride and delight.

"And here we are!" he exclaimed, turning his palms up to indicate where they were. "Husband and wife. And I am married to the most beautiful, exciting woman imaginable. A woman out of time and fable. A woman about whom poems are made and civilizations built and destroyed. Deidre. Cressida. Guinevere. Cleopatra. Ramona."

"Helen of Troy," offered Nell.

"Yes. Sweet Helen."

Hammer sat up straighter and took on an expression of great seriousness.

"Now this is just an overview, you understand. I am counting on you, Nell Bane, to fill in the details. The color.

The conversation. Counting on you to make Ramona's story come alive and sing!"

Nell rubbed her jaw. A strange feeling was creeping along her spine. She was a little dubious.

"Fictionalize Ramona's story, do you mean?" she said. "Is that what you want? And is that exactly...um, well,... fair?"

Stuart Hammer hurried to assure her that it was completely fair. He wanted drama. Excitement! He wanted the word portrait of Ramona O'Hara to leap off the page with sizzling honesty.

"Oh, what have I gotten myself into this time?" Nell asked herself when, a few minutes later she was pushing through the doors of Burton Hall and into the twilight of a November evening.

The plug had recently been pulled on daylight savings time and what would have been a pleasant sunset dusk a week ago was unexpectedly darkened by the later hour and the gray weather. The rain had stopped though. That was a mercy, and Nell, shivering, trod on leaves sodden as cornflakes in the bottom of a cereal bowl, as she hurried toward the parking lot.

Chapter 9

"How goes it?" was Bunty Whitney's greeting when Nell drifted wanly into her studio. Then, looking at her friend, Bunty answered her own question.

"Uh-oh. Not great I gather."

"Are you in the middle of something?" Nell asked. "If you take a break it won't cause any clay to dry out, I hope."

"I'm not working on the wheel. Just mixing some glaze. What's up?"

Nell issued a bellows-worthy sigh.

"I'm not sure," she said. "Stuart Hammer has told me Ramona's story—or the gist of it anyway—and he wants me to weave the raw threads of it into prose worthy of a wildly passionate romance novel."

"Well?"

"Several problems," Nell sighed. "He's provided a general story line but he hasn't supplied the details I really need. Could I write a hot, bodice-ripper? Sure, but I'd have to invent most of it and then it would be a piece of fiction. It wouldn't truly be

Ramona O'Hara's story. Frankly, fiction isn't what I do."

"I can offer sympathy," Bunty said. "And I can even offer tea. But beyond tea and sympathy, I'm not going to be much help. I don't know nuthin' 'bout fiction writing—or even ghostwriting, so I'm afraid you're on your own, chum."

Nell sighed again.

"I was afraid of that," she said. And she wafted out the door of Bunty's studio and drifted across the backyard to her own back door.

Nell switched on the digital recorder and listened once again to Stuart Hammer's enthusiastic narration of his wife's life story. She tried to figure out what he wanted. Or expected. Or more to the point, what he needed. And the bonus question was why?

It seemed to her that Hammer perceived his wife as a romantic heroine—a woman who had come up from poverty, had escaped a drunken father's abuse and an uncle's incestuous advances. Ramona's beauty and charm had caught the attention of a film director who had cast her in a film and made her a minor movie star. She had made her way to America, as many of her countrymen had, in search of a better life. She had worked hard to earn it, willingly tending bar until late into the night to earn enough to put herself through classes at UMass. And like a princess in a fairy tale, she had met and married her prince—Professor Stuart Hammer, an unlikely prince indeed although the sole heir to the Has-Bean fortune—and she was living happily-ever-after in his mansion in Ipswich.

What did Hammer want? Well, he *seemed* to want to immortalize Ramona—to capture her in a nearly life-size oil portrait, and not content with that, he wanted to have to a story about his princess. A story that would narrate her romantic life.

But would the story be a biography? Or would it be a fairy

49

tale?

Nell concluded that she'd figured out most of Stuart Hammer's wish, but she wasn't sure she could carry out her assigned part.

Chapter 10

"Brrr..." Nell shivered as she let herself in the Fitzmaurice's side door and slammed it behind her. "Every fall I forget what winter's going to feel like," she complained. "It's warm in here though. Have you got a fire going?"

"Yes," Ann Fitzmaurice said. "Go have a warm and I'll pour a couple of coffees. Your blood's still thin, that's your trouble. I haven't seen much of you lately. Been wondering how it's going with Stuart Hammer's project."

"It's a long story," Nell said, "and that's partly why I'm here—to vent. How is *your* project going?"

"Pretty well, actually."

Ann was wearing a blue cashmere sweater and her hair was tied back with a black ribbon. Nell thought she looked quite smart.

"Have a look," Ann invited.

And Nell did. She stepped lightly to the other end of the room and drew a sharp breath when she saw the canvas. The smears of brown underpaint had been transformed into the figure of a seated woman turned almost three-quarters to the right. She wore a bathrobe-like garment of rich crimson and one fold of it was slipping sideways off her shoulder to reveal creamy skin. A cloud of dark hair tumbled in waves onto the bared shoulder, contrasting with the light skin and making it appear to glow."

Nell was overwhelmed.

"Oh, Ann!" she breathed. "It's magnificent."

Ann, with one of Bunty Whitney's coffee mugs cradled in her hands, came to Nell's side. She regarded the portrait with some satisfaction.

"I'm pretty pleased with it," she said. "I think I've caught a good likeness. Took some doing though."

She sipped her coffee and over the rim of the mug, continued to regard her work.

Nell couldn't draw her eyes away from the portrait.

"Is it finished?"

"Far from it," Ann said. "Ramona will come back for several more sittings and in between, I've have a lot of fiddly stuff to do."

"Has Stuart seen it?" Nell wanted to know.

"Not yet. He's coming next week for a viewing. It's been all I could do to keep him away. He keeps wanting to peek, so finally I told him that yes, he was invited to take a look at the portrait of Ramona."

"I wish I were doing as well as you." Nell's voice was wistful, and Ann, immediately alert, wanted to know what was wrong.

And so Nell began to tell the story of Stuart Hammer's expectation.

"Do you remember Rumplestiltskin?" she asked.

Ann looked bewildered for a few seconds.

"Grimm's fairy tale? That one? What about it?"

"Well, remember there was a maiden who was put in a room full of straw and ordered to spin it into gold. And the poor girl was distraught, as anyone faced with that impossibility would be. Then this ugly dwarf—Rumplestiltskin—appeared and said he'd perform the task for her and demanded as payment her firstborn child. Of course the silly girl promised, but what choice did she have?"

"So who are you?" Ann asked. "The maiden or Rumplestitlskin?"

Nell made a face at her.

"I'm the maiden, of course, and I've been ordered to spin straw into gold. Ordered by Stuart Hammer. He's given me straw. And not much of it either! Stuart won't permit me to talk with Ramona because he wants the story to be a *surprise*."

Both women were silent. Nell, contemplating the impossibility of her task and Ann radiating unspoken sympathy. Nell turned to look again at the portrait of Ramona.

"However..." she began cunningly, "... however, if I could just *see* Ramona O'Hara—observe her, you know—it would help a great deal."

Nell looked at Ann out of the corner of her eye.

"Do you and she talk during the painting sessions?" she asked.

"Not while I'm working," Ann said, "but I give her a break every twenty minutes or so—it isn't easy being a model, you know. Sometimes it's hell to stay awake. And then too, something always itches and you're dying to scratch but you're afraid to move for fear of screwing up the artist's work. Well, away, we do chat a bit during the break. Why? Are you thinking what I'm thinking you're thinking?"

"Yep. Could I? Could I just sit in on one session? I'd sit in a corner and be quiet as a mouse."

Ann considered.

"I don't see how it could do any harm. I'll think up some plausible reason for you to be there, and I doubt Ramona would mind. She seems very easy going. Very tolerant of this portrait painting business, but I think she learned long ago to be tolerant of a number of Stuart Hammer's whims. A week from Thursday is our next scheduled session. Is that alright with you?"

"Listen, I'm grateful for any bits of straw I can get hold of," Nell said.

She felt considerably better. And she was enormously grateful to Ann Fitzmaurice for holding out this wisp. She planned to sit quietly, observing Ramona O'Hara—each nuance and each expression. And at the break, when she spoke, Nell would be able to hear Ramona's voice and this too would help as she wrote the story.

Chapter 11

But before Ramona's next sitting could take place, Nell heard again from Ann Fitzmaurice. And Ann was angry.

"I can't believe it!" She sputtered over the phone, quite forgetting to even say hello.

"Wait! Slow down!" Nell ordered. "I'm not even on the page. What are you talking about?"

"Stuart Hammer!" Ann spat the name like a curse.

"What? What's happened?"

"I'll tell you what's happened!" Ann snapped. "I told Stuart he could come and see the painting, although I warned him it was still a long ways from the finish. So fine. Stuart comes charging over before I've scarcely hung up the phone. In he comes and takes a look."

Ann stopped. For dramatic effect, Nell assumed.

"Yes. So?" she prodded.

"He doesn't like it!" Ann declared. She sounded furious.

Nell could hardly believe this. The portrait, as far as she could see, was exquisite.

"He *said*," Ann's voice twisted into sarcasm, "he *said* that the portrait didn't look like Ramona."

Nell was a bit at sea. She herself had never seen Ramona O'Hara—not even a photograph—and she was hardly in a position to insist that the painting was a dead ringer for the subject. But Ann had used the artist's term 'caught a likeness', and Nell had not doubted her. Moreover, Ann Fitzmaurice was highly critical of her own work and would never had made that claim if it were not so. Nell was puzzled.

"What are you going to do?" she wanted to know.

"I'll have to rework it," Ann answered pragmatically. She was calmer now.

"Can you do that?" Nell couldn't imagine how.

"Yes. I'll paint out some things and do some overpainting. Start again if I have it. But when you do that, there's always the danger of over-working the piece. Listen, are you still coming to Ramona's session on Thursday?"

Nell was.

"Good," said Ann grimly. "You can see her for yourself. Then *you* tell *me* whether or not the portrait resembles Ramona O'Hara."

Chapter 12

Ann Fitzmaurice had provided a small but comfortable chair for Nell in a corner of her studio and had offered Ramona a casual introduction.

"This my friend Nell Bane. She's writing an article on North Shore occupations and she wanted to include an artist, so I've agreed to let her sit in on a portrait session. Perhaps I should have discussed this with you, Ramona, but I figured you wouldn't mind."

Ramona O'Hara didn't mind. She had simply smiled at Nell and given a "whatever" shrug.

"Fine with me," she'd said.

And so Nell was free to relax—she'd been oddly tense, fearing Ramona's rejection—and now she could settle comfortably back in her chair. She hoped she looked calm but every fiber was attuned. Vibrating. Ready to vacuum up any impression or scrap of information that would reveal Ramona O'Hara.

"You husband looked at the painting," Ann told Ramona.

"I thought I'd captured a good likeness but he wasn't pleased, so I'm going to have to make some adjustments. I don't yet know if they will be minor or major, so I hope you'll bear with me."

Ramona O'Hara smiled. Her smile, Nell thought, was transformational. Her face, indeed her whole aspect, changed. Radiated energy. Charm.

"That sounds like Stuart," she said. But she didn't expand on her comment, and Nell, waiting breathlessly, was disappointed. Had this been an interview or one of her information-collecting sessions, Nell would have pounced on that offhand comment like a robin on an earthworm. She would have guided, cadged, niggled or winkled very subtly until Ramona enlarged upon the comment and revealed more information about Stuart. She would have guided Ramona down a discursive path to reveal what Stuart was like. She squirmed a bit in her chair and bit her tongue to keep silent.

Ann tranquilly applied her brushes to the canvas. She was holding two—rather like chopsticks—and painting with a third. Every so often she'd jab the brush-of-the-moment into her fist and pluck out one of the others and go at the canvas again, Silence reigned. Somewhere in the bowels of the Fitzmaurice house an appliance—a boiler or a water heater—made itself known. The Fitzmaurice's antique grandfather clock deeper in the house woke and carried out its required annunciation with a series of mellow bongs.

Silence returned.

Nell's gaze drifted from the canvas to the subject in the chair. Ramona O'Hara, with remarkable ease, had settled into the pose she had been assigned. Ann had given her a few directions—"Lower the shoulder just here. Yes, that's right, slip the robe off the shoulder just a little more. Tilt the chin down and away. Eyes focus here, yes just here. Yes. I want to see that jawline."

Ann painted on, working rapidly. Nell, glancing at the canvas, was surprised to see Ann working in colors that clashed. Jarring, impossible colors that Nell couldn't even see in the subject, but then—brush scrubbing furiously—Ann blended the outrageous pigments, and Nell would never have known that a shade of lurid purple could turn so soft and shadowy.

Nell regarded the model. Was Ramona O'Hara beautiful? Nell decided she really couldn't say. Arresting, that was one of the adjectives Nell might have used. Dramatic? Certainly. Romantic? That was apparently how Stuart Hammer saw his wife, but was that accurate? Nell didn't know. And the original question remained suspended in her mind: was Ramona O'Hara beautiful?

With a tired-sounding sigh, Ann Fitzmaurice laid her brushes in the tray below the canvas.

"We can take a break, Ramona," she said. "I need to get the kinks out and I'll bet you could use something. Coffee? A soft drink?"

"The powder room, I think," replied Ramona O'Hara. She stood and as a cat might, stretched. "And a glass of water would revive me."

She pulled the descendant flap of robe over her naked shoulder and padded off to the Fitzmaurice's powder room.

Ann looked at Nell.

"What do you think?"

"Well. First I think you did catch a likeness. A remarkable one, and I can't for the life of me think what Stuart Hammer is complaining about."

But before Nell could enlarge on this, Ramona was back. At the kitchen sink, she ran the tap, filled a glass and sipped gratefully. She turned to Nell.

"Ann said you're writing an article. So you must be a writer."

Hearing her own words, she laughed.

"Duh. That's pretty obvious, isn't it? Who's the article for? North Shore Magazine?"

Nell smiled, and she intended to avoid the pitfalls of both questions.

"I write for a number of publications," she said neutrally. "But speaking of occupations, please tell me, how do you like being an artist's model?"

Ramona O'Hara shrugged.

"It's not something I'd like to do as an occupation. Too static. Sort of boring. But this one-time experience is a novelty and so it's mildly interesting. And it's interesting as well to see yourself as someone else sees you and to see that vision translate to a canvas."

This speech surprised Nell. She realized suddenly that she had pre-judged Ramona O'Hara—hadn't expected her to be so articulate. She'd had unreasonable expectations and since Nell didn't like to see that tendency as part of her dossier, she felt ashamed.

"I've never had the experience you describe," she admitted. "You've made me a little envious."

Ann crooked an eyebrow.

"Any time you want to sit for a portrait, sweetie, I can be ready. It'll cost you though."

Nell grinned.

"That's what I was afraid of." She pretended to sigh sadly. "I'll just have to find a sugar daddy to foot the bill."

Nell gulped guiltily. Now you've done it! she scolded herself. That's a terrible thing to say. But Ramona didn't seem offended at all. She laughed in fact.

"It helps," she said and resumed her pose on the chair,

pushing the robe slightly off her shoulder as she did so. "Is this the pose, Ann?"

"A little more to the left," Ann directed, "and lower the chin—yes. There. You've got it."

Nell settled back to her chair to observe some more, but a half hour had barely passed when a phone rang.

"Rats!" exclaimed Ann. She fished her cell out of her apron pocket and glanced at its face.

"Oops. I've got to take this call. I'll be quick as I can. Ramona, you can take another break."

Ann hurried down the hall to a deeper part of the house. "What did you find out?" they heard her say before she faded out of earshot. Ramona came out of her pose the way a cat comes out of the sun. She smiled, and Nell saw her chance to strike up a conversation.

"Your name," Nell said, finding her way carefully. "You're Irish?"

" 'Fraid so."

"What part of Ireland are you from?"

Ramona looked slightly confused. "Part? Oh, I'm not *from* Ireland. My mother is though. Or was."

If Ramona O'Hara had dashed a pan full of cold water into Nell's face, she couldn't have been more startled. She felt like she'd just been pushed over a cliff and was scrabbling to recover and gain a grasp, a toe-hold, anything to pull her back to stable ground.

Ramona was watching her curiously.

"I thought Ann said," Nell stammered, "rather she might have mentioned... that you'd been born in Ireland. Or I must have just assumed it. Sorry. You know what they say," she added apologetically, "assume makes an ass out of you and me."

"I was born in Boston City Hospital," Ramona said matter-of-factly. "In Southie."

Then it was Ramona's turn to ask a question.

"So what sort of writing do you do, Nell?"

Nell decided to moderate her standard answer to this question.

"Generally I write whatever anyone is ready to pay me for, so that can cover a pretty broad territory. Memoir. Biography. That's the usual run, but I've done other things too."

"Sorry about that." Ann came sailing back into the room. "Couldn't be helped. Okay, Ramona, back into position!"

Ramona had grown practiced at assuming the pose Ann wanted, and she shifted in her chair and presented the desired profile.

Ann painted. Nell and Ramona sat in silence. And as she sat, Nell mentally replayed her exchange with Ramona O'Hara, hardly believing what she'd heard. She started doubting herself. Had she heard correctly? Nell reviewed the conversation again. No, she'd heard it right. Ramona was not from Ireland. She'd been born in South Boston—in Boston City Hospital, as a matter of fact.

The old Boston City ... Nell's mind reeled off on a thread of its own. The hospital had been a fixture in the South Boston community since the 1800s, and Southie residents depended on its services and its charity. It had closed around 1966. Well, not closed exactly—merged—merged with Boston University to become Boston Medical Center. Nell had a friend who was at BU during the merger, and Ellie had found the whole procedure annoying and inconvenient. She had complained endlessly about it to Nell and to anyone else who would listen.

Boston City was the poor relation in the merger. It's reputation as the hospital for the poverty-stricken took a while to disappear, but even now, people of Nell's vintage associated the old Boston City with the indigent and uninsured. So Ramona O'Hara had been born right there, and Carrach Duh—

somewhere west of Galway, Castlebar and Carrowbeg—didn't feature in her curriculum vitae at all.

Ann sighed finally and put her brushes down.

"I'm exhausted," she declared, "and you must be too, Ramona. Want a cup of tea before you go?"

Nell was hoping Ramona would say yes to the tea. She wanted the opportunity to winkle out a few more clues to what Ramona O'Hara's story really was, but this was denied her. Ramona had to scoot. Or claimed she did. She turned to Ann with a smile as she shrugged into her coat.

"Thank you for your patience with Stuart," she said. "He can be a bit obsessive. Well, I hope Himself will be better satisfied with today's results. I expect he'll be around post haste to have a look. Good luck."

"Good luck indeed," Ann murmured as they watched Ramona go up the path to the Fitzmaurices' little car park and to her car.

Chapter 13

Nell, sorting soup recipes, made a confusing discovery. There were two recipes for asparagus soup, and while they were similar, they definitely weren't the same.

"Now why do I have two?" she asked herself.

"I suppose," she answered herself, "because one is better than the other."

But which was the winner? She reread both recipes and each seemed to have value. Well, there was one way to find out. Have a side-by-side competition. And this, she decided would give her a chance to invite some favorite judges. A phone call to Robert Hutchins, who, in consultation with his partner Jerry Gasso, set a lunch date. Next Nell called Bunty Whitney.

"A judge in an asparagus soup contest?" Bunty repeated. "Never done that but it's a line item I'll be able to cross off my bucket list."

"Come on, Bunty," Nell chided. "That's never been on your bucket list! What *is* on your bucket list, by the way? See the sunrise over Mount Kilamanjaro? Hike to the top of Manchu

Pichu. Stand on China's Great Wall?"

"Naw! Let's see ... go to the roller derby. That's definite. Very high on the list. There's this whole culture to it."

"The roller derby!" Nell exclaimed. "Come on! Really?"

"Yes, really." Bunty was put out by Nell's surprise—or maybe by her shock. "The Boston Derby Dames have a traveling league. They appear all around the area. I've read all about them. The Wicked Pissahs ... The Cosmonaughties. Dying to go. Want to come?"

"Well, I'll think about it ..." Nell hedged.

"You do that," Bunty said briskly. "Listen, I gotta go and write Asparagus Soup on my bucket list so I can cross it off after the contest."

ASPARAGUS SOUP: Version One
1-1/2 pounds asparagus, peeled and cut bite-size
2 T butter
2 medium onions, chopped
6 cups chicken broth
zest of one lemon
3/4 cup heavy cream
Cook the asparagus in salted water until just tender. Drain and chill. Cook the onion in the melted butter until just soft, then add the chicken broth and lemon zest. Bring the mixture just to the boil, reduce to simmer and add the asparagus, then the cream. Use the immersion blender to make a smooth soup. Serve warm or chilled.

ASPARAGUS SOUP: Version Two
1 bundle of asparagus
1/2 of a large, sweet onion
6 cups of chicken stock
1/2 cup Greek yogurt

Smoked paprika

Pepper

Cut the heads off the asparagus stalks. Combine half the asparagus heads with the onion and stock in a pan. Reserve the remaining heads and set aside. Tie the asparagus stalks together and add it to the pan. Bring the ingredients to the boil and simmer for one hour. Discard the stalks. Add the reserved asparagus heads to the stock. Blend in the yogurt and season to taste. Serve warm or chilled with a smoked paprika garnish.

Nell prepared a green salad and pushed a pan of popovers into a hot oven. So she was all set when Robert Hutchins and Jerry Gasso, looking hungry, burst through the door, followed almost at once by Bunty Whitney, who from her studio window had seen them arrive.

Chapter 14

"Stuart Hammer is coming over this afternoon."

Ann Fitzmaurice's voice on the phone had sounded rather desperate Nell thought.

"Please say you'll come too!" Ann had pleaded.

Nell had been planning to do some shopping for Robert Hutchins's birthday next week, but she recognized a plea when one came, and she put off the shopping excursion and warmly assured Ann she would be there.

"I need a witness," Ann had explained. "I need you to listen to what Stuart says and perhaps to validate my perception. Or else to tell me outright that I am off the mark—that the work-in-progress isn't catching Ramona's likeness."

And so Nell was standing once again the Fitzmaurices' kitchen with Ann when Stuart Hammer's car rolled into the car park. They watched him approach.

"Nell!" he said with pleasure as he came in the door. "You're here too. What a nice surprise."

Stuart Hammer stood expectantly in the kitchen, beaming

and rocking from heel to toe and back again.

"Let me take your coat, Stuart," Ann said politely. "And may I get you anything to drink. Tea? Water? Perhaps a glass of sherry?"

But no, Stuart only wanted one thing—a look at Ramona's portrait. And so Ann, with a graceful sweep of her arm, indicated that he was welcome to step towards the easel.

Released—given permission—Stuart Hammer almost bolted to the studio. Ann and Nell remained in their places, observing him closely. But once he was standing in front of the canvas, the look of transport slowly faded from Stuart's face and was replaced by a one of deep thought and consideration. He cupped his chin in his left hand, his forefinger tap-tap-tapped against his nose, and his right arm, tight against his chest, supported his left elbow.

Minutes seemed to pass as he stood in contemplation, and the longer he stood there, the more Nell could feel Ann's affect deflate.

Stuart finally spoke.

"I am puzzled," he said slowly, "that the woman—that *figure* in the painting—is so ordinary," and he pointed his tapping finger at the canvas, "whereas Ramona—*Ramona* is *beautiful*. Extraordinary."

He turned to Ann with an accusatory look.

"I can't understand how you don't see that," he said reproachfully.

"Stuart," Ann said gently, coming to stand next to him. "I paint what I see. Does it not look like Ramona to you?"

"Oh, it looks like her," he conceded. "but ... it's just that the portrait lacks—I don't know what you'd call it—passion, I guess. Yes, passion and romance and all the vibrancy that Ramona brings to life. You just painted a *woman*! A flat picture of an ordinary woman."

"Nell!" he suddenly ordered. "Come here! Tell us what you think."

And Nell obediently stepped over to join them. She allowed a few moments to given the impression she was studying the painting.

"I think she's caught a good likeness," Nell admitted.

"Of course, you've never seen Ramona!" Hammer scoffed. "How can you tell?"

"True, point taken," Nell admitting, lying slightly. "But I see a very dramatic portrait of a woman. A strong woman. An attractive woman."

"But not a ravishing beauty," Stuart insisted. "My Ramona is ravishing! This woman is just ordinary."

He turned to Ann.

"You can fix this, can't you? Make some change, do something to catch what Ramona actually looks like—you can do that can't you?"

"I can try," Ann said humbly.

And Nell felt bad for her and for the untenable position her friend was in. Moreover, she felt Stuart was being unreasonable, and she couldn't imagine what more Ann could do. Nell had seen both Ramona and the portrait, and Ann, in her opinion, couldn't have gotten a greater likeness if she'd used a camera.

Stuart Hammer apparently felt comfortable again, and he turned away from the portrait and looked at Nell.

"And how is your project coming along?" he asked. "Our portrait of Ramona drawn in words?"

"A little slower than I'd expected," Nell admitted. "I had hoped for more grist for the mill, you could say. More detail to work with."

But Stuart Hammer apparently didn't want to hear that.

"You'll be fine," he assured her. "But I do hope to see a

first draft fairly soon. Well, ladies, I will bid you good day and leave you to your respective challenges. Call me, Ann, as soon as you have the portrait in condition for me to see it."

And Stuart Hammer, with a cheery little mock salute, buttoned his coat and stepped out the door.

"Jesus Christ!" said Ann Fitzmaurice when the door closed.

"I'll second that," Nell said unhappily.

Chapter 15

Nell was supposed to be writing. She was supposed to be writing about Ireland, and she had collected a pile of maps, travel brochures and descriptions of the Irish countryside. This, she hoped, would help her describe the country northwest of Galway and Castlebar, Carrowbeg and Carrach Duh. Was a black bog actually black? She wasted a number of perfectly good minutes wondering about this.

Nell learned that Irish was still widely spoken in the area of Ramona's birth. Or what was, according to Stuart Hammer, the area of Ramona's birth. She wondered if Irish was widely spoken in Southie.

She'd checked the facts about Spanish Armada shipwrecks and had determined that the story of the Black Irish was largely myth, albeit an extremely popular one. She had made a list of pub names and even, in some desperation, made a list of Irish beers, stouts and ales. And she had applied her fingers to the keyboard and tried to write. She'd started—and aborted—sentence after sentence, paragraph after paragraph, and the words just petered out, leaving Nell staring at a blank computer screen.

She had tried writing about the Irish countryside, driveling on about the mists and the moors and the lush landscape done up in seventeen shades of green. And her own words disgusted her.

She stood up and paced.

She thought about her list of Irish brews and remembered the taste of Guinness. Molasses, that's what Guinness reminded her of. She really needed to write molasses on her shopping list because her recipe for gingerbread called for a whole cup of molasses, and a nice gingerbread was quick to make and useful to have on hand in the cold weather.

And cold weather, yes. A time for soups and stews. Excellent cold weather dishes. Perhaps she should make an Irish stew. Or better yet, she could make Irish stout soup if she could find that recipe. Yes, that might put her in the mood to write Ramona's story. Of course, you couldn't have an authentic Irish stew or stout soup without Guinness.

Nell wondered if she had any Guinness in the house. Maybe there was some down cellar.

But there wasn't. She looked. Twice.

Now Nell had a reason to leave the maps and travel folders, the papers and unresponsive computer and go out for some supplies. She certainly needed molasses, although not for the soup. For that, she'd need Guinness and some good beef also. And were there enough carrots? Better restock those as well.

Stuart Hammer's story about Ramona O'Hara could wait one more day. Now where was that recipe? The stout soup was nearly of a stew consistency, but it had all the excellent points of a pot of soup on a winter day—rich, meaty flavor, vegetables and a savory broth. Nell pulled out the recipe for Irish Stout Soup.

IRISH STOUT SOUP
2 pounds lean stewing beef
3 T canola oil
2 T flour
Salt and freshly ground pepper and a pinch of cayenne
2 large onions, coarsely chopped
1 large clove garlic crushed (optional)
2 T tomato puree, dissolved in 4 tablespoons water
1-1/4 cups Guinness stout
2 cups carrots, cut into chunks
Sprig of thyme
Salt, pepper, cayenne
Chopped parsley for garnish

Nell trimmed the beef and cut it into 2-inch cubes. She tossed the beef in a bowl of seasoned flour—1 T of flour, salt, pepper and a pinch or two of cayenne. Then she added the oil and tossed it again.

Next she heated the remaining oil in a wide pan over a high heat and browned the meat on all sides, removing the pieces as they browned and began to stick to the pan. She added the onions to the pan, covered it and cooked it gently for about 5 minutes the onions. Then she uncovered the pan to let the onions brown a bit and flung the carrots in to brown as well. Then in went the garlic and puree. Nell scraped the mixture into a soup pot and deglazed the browning pan with a good splash of Guinness, stirring to caramelize the meat juices. She poured this over the vegetables in the soup pot and added the beef as well along with the juices that had seeped from the beef during the standing time. Finally, the remaining Guinness went into the pot along with thyme. Nell tasted for salt and added a pinch. Then she covered the pot and let the stout soup simmer very gently until the meat was tender. This, Nell expected, would take 2 to 3 hours, at which point she would taste, correct the seasonings and scatter a lot of chopped parsley on the top.

Once this was done though, and the soup was simmering, there was nothing for Nell to do but return to the computer and the piles of Irish trivia and begin trying try once more to spin straw into gold.

Chapter 16

I'm hoping to reach Nell Bane," the woman's voice said. "Am I in luck?"

"You are indeed," Nell said, "and to whom am I speaking?"

"Ramona O'Hara. I asked Ann if you lived in Newburyport, then I got your number from information. Nell, I have something I'd like to discuss with you. A project. And I'm wondering if would it be possible for me to come to your house?"

Mystified, Nell said that would be fine. Then, after hanging up the phone, she began to grow uneasy. She couldn't imagine what Ramona O'Hara could want with her. She put in a call to Ann Fitzmaurice, but Ann was as bewildered as she. And no, Ann hadn't mentioned the secret project Nell was doing for Stuart.

Nell fumed. She didn't like secrets. Secrets always came back to bite you in the backside. And to prove it, all you had to do was look at Stuart Hammer's secret—the one he'd made Nell swear to keep. The secrecy was making her feel guilty.

Suspicious. Just look! An innocent call from someone had thrown her into a panic of paranoia. And to compound these feelings, Nell was getting angry. But there was nothing to do but wait for Ramona's visit and see what would happen next.

Ramona O'Hara claimed she'd had no trouble at all following Nell's directions to the little antique cape. Nell, well experienced with the confusing lanes that wound through Newburyport's back neighborhoods, had a little trouble believing Ramona's claim, but she put on a welcoming smile.

"The kitchen is the brightest spot in this house," Nell told her guest, "and coffee is all set to be brewed. I just have to flick the switch, if coffee sounds good to you, that is."

It did. And as the fragrant brew dripped into the carafe, Ramona O'Hara looked all about the kitchen, touching the marble counter almost reverently.

"My goodness, I've never seen a stove quite like that."

"It's an Aga," Nell said. "A great splurge, but a client of mine was so pleased with his memoir, that he landed me with a handsome bonus check—a check that I lost no time spending on this Aga Companion. It's just the junior size Aga, but I'd always been dying to own one."

"Just black," Ramona said, when Nell handed her the mug of coffee and gestured toward the snug at the end of the kitchen. And once seated on the sofa with Ramona across from her in the club chair, Nell cupped her own mug in both hands and waited for Ramona to come to the reason for the visit. Hammer's secret felt to her like a third entity in the room. She felt like "Secret" was flashing on her forehead where Ramona could read it. Nell felt resentful. Also nervous

But it turned out that, no, Ramona was apparently unaware of her husband's commission. She wanted to see Nell on quite a different matter.

"I remember you said that you generally write whatever a

client wants," she said. She raised her eyebrows questioningly.

"Pretty much, yes," Nell agreed. She relaxed a bit. "I do draw the line at pornography, and I don't write poetry either. What do you have in mind?"

"I am thinking of starting a little business," Ramona said. "A massage business, and I need a brochure. Just a trifold thing that explains the services and all. But I have no idea how to go about it—how to approach it. Have you ever done that sort of writing?"

Nell suffered a flashback to her days as an advertising copywriter—days she was just as glad to have behind her— but she knew she could handle Ramona's assignment with one hand tied behind her back. Well...no... that wouldn't work because she'd need both hands for typing on the keyboard, but Ramona's job should be easy.

"I served a long indenture as a copywriter in an ad agency," Nell said. "It's been quite a while since I've written and designed a trifold brochure, but I used to do dozens of them. Taking on another one would be like riding a bicycle."

Ramona O'Hara looked confused.

Nell laughed. "You never forget how to ride it," she explained.

Nell suddenly realized that working with Ramona would carry a bonus that her new client couldn't know. As they worked together, Nell would be able to observe Ramona more closely. Could have conversations with her and could therefore learn more about the subject of Stuart's commission. And perhaps she could also satisfy some of her own Pandora-like curiosity about the disconnect between Stuart's story and Ramona's.

"So tell me about your idea," Nell said warmly. "A massage business—interesting. Tell me why you want to organize this start-up. Where is the business is going to be? What is it to be called? Tell me about your business plan and your goals. Tell me about your services."

"My goodness," Ramona blinked. "All that? Well, I guess I can answer all those questions. But it'll take some time."

"Time is what I've got a-plenty," Nell said, sitting back complacently against the cushion of the sofa in the snug. She smiled. Yes indeed, this would be a double opportunity.

Chapter 17

Nell hadn't forgotten how to ride a bicycle apparently. Or how to write a trifold brochure either.

"Why do you want to start a business?" she had asked Ramona. She did not say what she was thinking, that money was certainly no issue in the Has-Bean mansion.

A faraway look had come into Ramona's eyes and she had gazed toward Nell's kitchen window and somewhere into the late winter landscape outside.

"I've always worked," she answered slowly. "Until I married Stuart, that is, and I liked it. I liked feeling self-sufficient. Liked building my own destiny and being responsible for myself."

She seemed to be reading a script or prompter outside the window. Nell restrained herself from turning around to look.

"Stuart was adamant though, about my not working. He especially didn't want me tending bar. Meeting men. I think Stuart was jealous of the men I talked to in the Bowsprite—the place where we met."

Ramona came back to the present with a suddenness that was almost a bump. She looked directly at Nell.

"I want to create something new."

No, Ramona O'Hara was not, and never had been, a licensed massage therapist. That would be no problem though; she would simply hire therapists, being very "choosey" she said about the personalities of the women she'd hire.

Yes, she had found the perfect space for the business. It was down in Beverly, not far from the Bowsprite, actually. It was presently vacant but the rent was right and the location was super. A couple coats of paint, some carpet and furniture, put in the phone and she'd be all set. All she needed was a sign and some advertising. Hence, the trifold brochure.

And yes, she had a business name all picked out. Tenderly. That was it. What did Nell think?

Nell didn't know what she thought.

"Um..." she said, thinking madly, "it's not very descriptive, is it, the name? I mean Tenderly could mean anything. It could describe peas, for goodness' sake."

But that was the beauty of the name, Ramona asserted. It left something to the imagination. It was mysterious and mystical and at the same time soft, like a loving touch.

"See, I will have the song *Tenderly* playing softly in the background," she explained. "*The evening breeze, caressed the trees, ten-der-ly...* And all the colors in the place will be soft and pastel. Misty-like." Ramona hummed a few bars of the song, then began to sing softly, "*The shore was kissed by sea and mist, ten-der-ly.*"

Nell nodded. "Mist," she repeated. "Got it."

This, she told herself, was her client and the client was paying her—Nell—to write some copy. Rather obscure copy, Nell gathered, since Ramona didn't seem to want her massage business described in too much detail.

"Can you write something up?" Ramona wanted to know. "Sort of put it in a trifold design?"

Nell assured her that she could. But as Ramona stood and slipped into her coat, Nell had one last question.

Ramona's chin came up.

"No," she answered firmly. "No, I do not intend to tell my husband about the business. And if you run into him at Ann's house, you must not tell him about it either."

For the second time, Nell swore to keep another's secret.

Chapter 18

"I don't understand it," Ann Fitzmaurice was saying. She sounded genuinely puzzled, but Nell heard a note of bitterness too. Ann was hurt by Hammer's criticisms and frustrated about her inability to satisfy him.

"I mean, Ramona O'Hara is a nice-looking woman," she continued, "but she's no raving beauty. Yet Stuart carries on as if she's a sought-after cover model for Vogue. Ravishing, he calls her. Exquisite!"

They were in 10 Center Street—one of Newburyport's upscale restaurants—and Nell and Bunty Whitney had been listening to Ann vent for quite a while. Bunty, Nell noticed, had drained her wine glass and was gripping the stem in a rather desperate way.

Nell had an inspiration.

"Did you ever read *Gone With The Wind*, Ann?"

"Read it? The summer I was in the eighth grade I practically ate it! I pinched the book from my mother's bookcase and read it straight through. Then I went back and started reading it over. For years I could recite great swatches of it from memory."

"Then you'll remember how it begins," Nell said.

She closed her eyes for a moment to retrieve the first sentence of the Margaret Mitchell classic.

"*Scarlett O'Hara was not beautiful,*" she recited, "*but men seldom realized it when captured by her charm as the Tarleton twins were now.*"

Ann was smiling.

"I read it too," Bunty said, grinning. "Big old brown book. I stole my mother's copy too, and when she found out, she had a fit. Thought I was too young for such racy reading."

"I wanted nothing more than to look like Scarlett," Ann reminisced.

"You mean," Bunty told her, "you wanted to look like Vivian Leigh in the movie role of Scarlett. Wasn't she something? Those green eyes glittering like glass and that precise little cat's chin! What a flirt! I, however, wanted nothing more than to be swept up the staircase in the arms of Rhett Butler."

She laughed and Ann, remembering, smiled fondly.

"Well," Nell continued, looking at Ann. "it seems to me that we have something similar happening here. Think about it. Ramona O'Hara may not be beautiful but doesn't she have a captivating charm? Some elemental magnetism?"

"Oh Lord," said Ann, "and I just realized—O'Hara! Do you suppose that's a coincidence?"

"There are no coincidences," Bunty Whitney intoned ominously.

"Well, whatever." Nell was interested in examining the issue further. "The problem as I see it is that when Stuart Hammer looks at Ramona, he is seeing something very different from the person we see."

"Well," Ann offered, "she is his wife—perhaps he's too

close to be objective."

"Sounds plausible," Nell agreed. "Bunty, do you have an opinion?"

"I've never met either of them." Bunty was pragmatic. "Any opinion I'd offer would be conjecture and merely academic."

She twirled her empty glass on the table, studying it as she appeared to think. Then she softened.

"Well, try this," she offered. "Would you say that Stuart Hammer loves his wife?"

The other two nodded.

"Would you say that he loves her passionately?"

"Yeah, I would say that," Ann affirmed. Nell nodded also.

"And would it be going too far to say that he idolizes her?" Bunty wanted to know.

Ann and Nell looked at each other. Then, when some invisible agreement was exchanged, they both looked at Bunty and nodded.

"Yes, that's a fair statement," Nell said.

"Then would you say," Bunty continued doggedly, " that he *idealizes* her. In other words, could he be so smitten that he could be in love with the *idea* of Ramona? Could he have created some impossible image of his love—some ideal—and that image is what he sees when he looks at her? I'd suggest it might be that *image* that he is in love with."

Bunty watched the expressions on her friends' faces, and then gave her diagnosis.

"Stuart Hammer might be in what is called 'thrall'."

"And so he is seeing beauty that may not really be there," Ann said slowly. "I think I'm beginning to see."

"*La Belle Dame sans Merci hath thee in thrall,*" murmured Nell.

"Exactly," Bunty said firmly. "And as long as he is in thrall, he is never going to see the reality of Ramona—the image that you or I would see when we look at her."

"Huh," Nell said. Then apologized. "That didn't sound very bright, I guess. So, Stuart is in thrall of Ramona. Or do you say *to* Ramona? What about it?"

"Are we ever going to order?" Bunty demanded. "I'm starving here. Look, let's order, then I'll give a little lecture on the psychological effects of thrall."

She leaned out of the booth and caught the waitress's eye.

When they had ordered—lemon balsamic chicken for Ann and Nell and the lobster mac and cheese for Bunty—and when the waitress had sashayed away to place the order, Bunty picked up her thread.

"It might be helpful to understand this," she said. "When you are in thrall to someone—enthrall—you are under their control. In a manner of speaking, you're a captive. You're totally subject to something else—some need or desire or appetite. Or some *one*. They are not controlling you though—the *condition* is. Thrall is like an addiction. Or perhaps like a disease."

She looked at Nell and Ann who were staring at her in fascination.

"What?" she demanded. "What's wrong? What have I said?"

"Go on, go on!" Nell instructed. "This is interesting."

"Well, that's about all there is to it," Bunty said. "Oh, except that thrall literally means slave or servant. It comes from the Old English."

Bunty buttered a piece of roll and chewed it complacently.

"This is what I don't understand," Nell said slowly. "You say Stuart, who is enthralled by Ramona—that is, in her thrall—is a captive. But it seems to me that Ramona is his captive. He has her under his thumb. He is making her do things that she may not want to do—like sit for a portrait. It sounds like he's trying to mold her into someone she isn't. So wouldn't you say that Ramona is in his thrall?"

But Bunty was firmly shaking her head.

"No. Don't you see? Ramona may be a captive, but she is a captive of another sort, not of a fantasy or an obsession. Look. Stuart Hammer idolizes Ramona O'Hara, but he also *idealizes* her—sees her as some sort of goddess when she is really just a pleasant, normally-attractive person. But he has created an idol, and he worships that idol. So he idealizes Ramona and he also idolizes her. In other words, he worships an idol but not necessarily the woman. And our salads are here and not a moment too soon."

Bunty picked up her fork in preparation for the salad to be set in front of her, and Nell knew the psychotherapist had concluded the session.

Bunty stabbed up a forkful of lettuce, looked up and smiled at her friends.

"Now! How 'bout those Patriots?"

Chapter 19

Jerry Gasso had invited Nell to take a sneak-peek tour of the house he was decorating on Beacon Hill. It wasn't an invitation he had to repeat twice. Nell was keen. She was present, front and center, at the Beacon Hill townhouse Jerry and Robert Hutchins shared, wearing her pearls, her best black coat and sensible boots for hiking over the Hill and traipsing through Jerry's project.

"Aren't you coming, Robert?" she asked.

Robert Hutchins was still wearing his reading glasses, and he bent to poke up the sitting room fire.

"I've already had the tour, and I'm waiting for Jerry to finish and announce the Big Reveal. These in-process things make me uneasy."

"He can't stand clutter and things being out of place," Jerry explained. "Robert likes to have everything tied down neatly. I, on the other hand, *adore* confusion. The opulence of chaos. The daring-do of tearing down walls! That's what sets my blood singing."

Robert Hutchins shook his head.

"Think of Shiva, the goddess of destruction," Jerry told him. "You have to tear down to built new. Die to the old, as it were."

"Run along, children," Robert said. "Have a good time. And watch your step, Nell. There may be loose boards and such that could give way and plunge you to the cellar."

Nell agreed wholeheartedly with Jerry Gasso though. It was exciting to tear down walls and bust through old bricks in order to insert new windows and let light come flooding in. Fenestration, Jerry called it. A lovely word. Nell adored it. After she and Lloyd had gone their separate ways, Nell couldn't wait to call in the designers and open up the elderly kitchen to the snug on one side and on the other side, to views of the back garden.

But she hadn't been prepared for the scale of Jerry's project. Sparing no expense, apparently, the politician and his wife had gutted the gracious old house. As Nell stood inside the front door, her eyes traveled up wonderingly.

"Jerry," she breathed, "how do you know where to begin?"

"At the beginning, my darling. It's very simple."

Nell was seeing Jerry Gasso in a new light, and she followed him through the house and up the staircases.

"The elevator will be just there," Jerry said, waving at nothing Nell could see. "It will be glass but the framework will be iron so it will be a juxtaposition of twenty-first century industrial-tech with an 1890s flavor."

"It's all so ... recent." Nell groped to describe her reaction. "I mean, I knew the place was gutted, but I somehow didn't dream you could streamline the interior of these old Federal places."

"Just wait" Jerry told her. "It will be very traditional-Louisburg Square on the outside. Passersby will think of worn

Persian carpets, soup tureens from old Canton and sherry decanters on Great Aunt Mabel's sideboard, but walk in the door and *wham*! It'll be Meet George Jetson."

He laughed.

"Now step into my sanctum sanctorum."

Jerry unlocked a paneled door and revealed a small room that was clogged with bolts of fabric, rolls of wallpaper, cans of paint and a few odd chairs draped in dust covers.

"This room is off-limits to the construction guys, and no one is allowed in except me and Beauticia."

"Beauticia!" Nell exclaimed. "Is that the wife's name?"

"Certainly not. It's Susan. But she doesn't mind when I call her Beauticia. She laughs."

Nell was fingering some of the fabrics.

"They're luscious," she said. "I'm envious."

"Hand-loomed linens," Jerry said, taking inventory, "silks, cut velvets, and look at this. You'd never believe this is outdoor fabric, but it can get soaked with rain on a patio and come inside to grace the best sofa in the house."

"Is there more?" Nell wanted to know.

"There will be," Jerry promised, "but for now you've seen the show. I'll invite you back for what Robert is calling the Big Reveal."

Back in the townhouse, Robert welcomed them with a friendly drinks tray and the request to hear Nell's report on the house. Her report was detailed and glowing. Jerry Gasso practically squirmed with pride.

"And what about your project?" Robert asked.

"Well," Nell said slowly. "It's beginning to look like there are two stories—two stories about the same woman. His and hers. I've heard the story according to Stuart Hammer, but I have yet to hear it from the subject's own lips."

Nell told them then, about Ann Fitzmaurice's difficulty

satisfying Hammer and her own confusion about Ramona's Irish roots. Robert frowned.

"Not a good sign," he murmured. "What do you think of this Stuart Hammer?"

"I think," Nell said, "that he is mildly, harmlessly crazy."

She laughed. But Robert Hutchins didn't. He was looking at her intently and his expression was grave.

"What makes you think he is harmless?"

"Oh Robert!" Nell gave an offhand flick with her wrist. "It's just a word I tossed off. I don't actually know that he's harmless anymore than I know he is crazy. Don't upset yourself."

"Harmless isn't a word you'd use casually, Nell. You are normally extremely precise with language. If you chose that word, there's a reason for it, even if it is a subconscious one."

Nell was annoyed.

"Ann and I already have Bunty Whitney psychoanalyzing for us, I don't need another shrink as well."

The accusation wasn't fair and Nell knew it. For one thing, Bunty hadn't volunteered her analysis—rather Ann and Nell had begged it out of her. And she knew her reaction to Robert wasn't fair either. Ordinarily, his remark would be have skated right off her like water hitting Teflon. So why was she so prickly? Did she suspect Robert might be right? Was there something unconscious that she was trying not to see?

"I'm sorry, Robert," she said. "Honestly. I wasn't right to get all huffy. And you are correct. I don't know if he's harmless, and, for that matter, I don't know if he's crazy either."

Robert continued to look levelly at her."

"You can be impetuous, Nell. Be careful."

Chapter 20

Nell was feeling the pressure of Stuart Hammer's last words.

"How is your project coming along?" he'd said. "Our portrait of Ramona drawn in words?"

As a matter of fact, it was hardly coming along at all. Nell had forced herself repeatedly to sit at the computer, but the hours there had sent her wandering distractedly through Google and she'd ended up trawling through eBay in search antique silver berry spoons. She'd read everything about Ireland she could get her hands on and had traveled virtually to Cannes to read about old film festivals. That had been a fool's errand! Her research turned up nothing about a talented Irish starlet named Ramona O'Hara, and now, in the light of what Nell now knew, it was no wonder!

She'd hoped that getting to know Ramona would serve up some useful material that she could parlay into the word portrait. And she *had* gotten a few things. She could honestly describe Ramona for instance, and she'd learned how Ramona spoke and the sound of her voice. But these were details that

Stuart had purposely withheld. How, then, could she use them in the portrait without rousing his suspicions?

Ramona's project, on the other hand, was ticking along with the precision of a bicycle's drive chain—everything meshing perfectly to move the vehicle along. Nell had met two more times with Ramona. First to show her a rough layout and copy for the trifold brochure for Tenderly, then again to present the final piece.

Ramona had been delighted, and to conclude their business, Nell had stood her client to a delightful luncheon at Loretta's where they'd been lucky enough to snag the table in the window alcove.

Nell picked up the tab for lunch and Ramona promptly handed over a check for the creative work on the trifold brochure.

"And how is the business going?" Nell asked.

"Swimmingly," Ramona told her proudly. "The lease is signed, the painters are coming on Thursday, and I've hired two very capable massage therapists and intend to interview a third tomorrow. I'm well underway."

Nell smiled. "And your husband? Has he gotten wind of this?"

Ramona made a wry face. "No, and there's no reason to think he will." She gave Nell a sharp look. "Unless somebody tells him..."

"If somebody does," Nell said, "it won't be me."

They had concluded lunch with coffee, and Nell played with her cup, using her index finger to turn the cup round and round by its handle.

"Secrets," she said. "Do they make you uncomfortable, Ramona?"

Nell's companion shrugged. "Not especially. Why? Do you have a problem with them?"

"As I matter of fact, I do. With some secrets anyway. Not all secrets, but some of them, come packaged up with ethical issues, and right now I find myself being held hostage by one such secret."

Ramona looked stricken.

"Oh, not yours!" Nell said hastily, reaching out to put her hand on Ramona's arm, "but there is another secret that is troubling me very much indeed."

And so, hating herself for it, Nell told Ramona about Stuart Hammer's commission, about the word portrait and about Stuart's insistence that it be kept a secret from Ramona.

At this last revelation, Ramona raised an eyebrow.

"Now, there!" Nell said. "I've violated a trust! Revealed a secret I promised to keep. But the thing is, Ramona, the story Stuart told me about you doesn't jibe with what I've learned about you firsthand. The versions just don't mesh."

Nell looked searchingly at her luncheon companion, but Ramona seemed inscrutable, her face a mask of calm expectancy. So Nell pressed on.

"Well, here's the ethical dilemma. On one hand, I promised Stuart to keep the word portrait under wraps until it was finished. Then it would be his to do whatever he wished with it. Publish it, present it to you tied in a red ribbon, whatever. I had no problem with that. The difficulty came when I began to discover that the material he was giving me for the portrait wasn't valid. It was some sort of make-believe, idealized fiction of his own devising. That realization put me—ethically speaking—in an uncomfortable position. I could honor my trust of silence and produce something I knew to be a lie, or I could violate the trust of silence in order to serve what I'd learned was the truth."

Nell sighed.

"The thing is, Ramona, knowing you as I have come to, I

can't see how I can hand over a fantastical portrait to Stuart."

Ramona sighed too.

"Stuart is a hopeless romantic," she said. "I can just image the b.s. he's fed you. So what are you going to do about it?"

"Do you have any suggestions?"

"None I can think of offhand."

"Well, here's one," Nell said. "What if I interview you at some length? Get your story. The real one. Then I'll blend the two versions as much as I can without compromising the truth. Maybe Stuart won't notice."

"Yeah," said Ramona O'Hara, "maybe he won't."

There was no conviction in her voice. "But, I guess it's worth a try."

Chapter 21

At Nell's suggestion, Ramona made several trips to Newburyport. Not to work on the trifold brochure, but this time to tell stories of her life. Nell listened, made notes and captured the narrations on her digital recorder. To her delight, several sessions with Ramona O'Hara yielded some extremely colorful material, and for the first time since meeting with Stuart Hammer in his office at Talcott, Nell was encouraged about drawing the word portrait of Ramona O'Hara. She played the recordings and sorted her notes and finally, like a hungry woman tucking into a favorite meal, she began to write the first draft.

She wrote late into the nights and rose early in the mornings. She had promised to show the draft to Ramona before presenting it to Hammer, and finally she determined it was right. Yes, she was pretty certain it was right.

Nell rose and stretched. She peered out the kitchen window at the setting sun that was industriously staining the sky to shades of rose madder and gold.

"I'm beginning to think like Ann Fitzmaurice," she murmured. "Talking in the vocabulary of pigments and colors. Now how to amuse myself next?"

She riffled through her soup recipes, searching for something she hadn't made in a while. And she was happily layering the ingredients of the soup into the casserole dish when Bunty Whitney strolled in.

"What're you making?"

Bunty was always curious.

"Soup," Nell replied. "Fish chowder."

"You're *baking* soup?" Bunty was incredulous.

"Yep."

"You're kidding." Bunty crowded closer for a view over Nell's arm. Nell arranged several generous pieces of haddock on the bed of potatoes and onions.

"This recipe has all the benefits," Nell explained. "It's fast, easy and delicious. It takes one hour to bake, so how would you like to share a glass of wine and stick around to try it?"

"I wouldn't want to miss it!" Bunty said.

Nell poured warm milk over the fish, sealed up the casserole with aluminum foil and slid it into the oven.

"I'm celebrating," she said as she brandished the corkscrew. "I finished up the draft of Ramona O'Hara's story about two hours ago, and it feels right. I'm going to see her on Friday."

"And then what?" Bunty wanted to know. "What are you going to do about that fairy tale that Stuart told you?"

"Huh."

Some of Nell's ebullience deflated. "That may be a bit tricky."

She sipped some wine and considered.

"I combed through his material and lifted whatever I could. Tried to weave it into Ramon's account, you know. With rather limited success, I have to say, but I did the best I could."

"Do you think he'll notice the differences?"

Nell shrugged. "Bound to, I guess. But there's nothing I can do about it except stick my neck out and try."

BAKED FISH CHOWDER
1 onion finely chopped
1 clove garlic, minced
2 large russet potatoes, diced
2 T butter
1 t salt
1 T fresh parsley, chopped
1 cup bottled clam juice
1-1/2 pounds haddock fillet, skinned
2 cups whole milk or cream, heated gently

Place the first seven ingredients in a shallow, buttered casserole dish. Place the fish on top of and cover the dish with a piece of aluminum foil. Bake at 350 degrees for 1 hour. Add the milk or cream and stir gently and flake the fish into bite-sizes bit with a fork.*

*Not liking the raw taste of onion in the soup, Nell gently sautéed the onion and garlic in 1 tablespoon of butter before adding it to the casserole.

Chapter 22

Nell was packing her briefcase. She paused just before inserting the manuscript and looked at it again. Then, distractedly, still reading, she backed up against a chair and sat down to read the manuscript one more time. She had used the first person voice after all. Told the story in Ramona's own voice. What would Stuart Hammer make of that?

Excerpt from
A Portrait of Ramona

The story starts, I suppose—*has* to start—with Mary Claire. Beautiful. Unpredictable. Funny. Promiscuous. Tragic. Impetuous. Passionate. Alcoholic. Red-haired. Temperamental. Musical. Well, a whole string of colorful adjectives could describe Mary Claire—all those words and more. The only adjective that could never apply was maternal. To all us kids— there were seven of us—she was never Mother, she was simply Mary Claire. Every time I hear the old Irish song *Wild Colonial*

Boy, I think of her. If there had been a wild colonial girl, she would have been named Mary Claire.

Mary Claire McCarthy turned her back on Ireland and County Mayo when she was sixteen. Left with a fight with her mother on her conscience and her brother's purloined wallet in her purse. A wallet that happened to contain a steamship ticket to New York. Little more than a year later she was Mary Claire Dargan, wife of Phillip Dargan, living in South Boston and pregnant. Her brother Danny caught up with her in Boston some time later and the family argument continued.

Personally, I never knew Dargan. He'd left the picture some years before I was born, although Mary Claire kept his name. Kept it right through the parade of men who lived with us in Southie, some of whom she actually married.

Southie. That was our home. And all us Dargan kids were passionate partisans of the town. We thought Southie was the best place in all the world, and we were ready to fight anyone who thought otherwise. Now, living in Ipswich and thinking of "over home", I can hardly image what we had to be so passionate about. Home was a series of flats in various projects—Old Colony, D Street, Old Harbor. Mary Claire changed addresses almost as often as she changed shoes, it seemed, but it was always within the projects. Always the projects. We never strayed beyond the limits of Southie. At times, during the busing troubles, for instance, the town seemed as war-torn and hate-filled as Belfast. But it was also familiar. Shopworn, it was, tired and even dangerous, its streets dirty, its buildings grimy, and Whitey Bulger riding around as king. Kids on the North Shore run and play in the woods. It was pretty much the same for us except our woods were buildings. The projects were our mazes and hideouts. Shouting to each other as we ran and played.

"Hey, I'm goin' down D. See yahs latah."

"Goin' down City Point.

"Goin' down G Street."

There were seven of us kids—I already said that—but only three of us are bona fide Dargans. Charmaine, Georgia and Joe. They are the oldest ones. Then there's Tommy—he's a Flynn. Michael and I come next —Jimmy O'Hara was our dad. And finally there's Marie Dawn, the youngest. Marie Dawn Costello.

After Dargan got out of the way, Mary Claire stopped keeping track of who had sired whom. In the maternity ward at Boston City, when they came around with the form and asked you to sign up the baby's name, Mary Claire took the easy road. She just assigned the man-of-the-hour's name to the new baby, and after that the baby got folded into the pack that the rest of Southie knew as "the Dargans".

Marie Dawn, though, she took her name and her situation personally. Mary Claire was having a brief relationship with a man named Buddy Costello when Marie Dawn arrived. She'd only known Buddy for two months before the baby came and she kicked him out four weeks after, but she landed the baby with the name Costello even though Buddy hadn't been around nine months earlier. Said she liked the name. It sounded Italian. Buddy Costello had a brogue thick enough to be sliced for Kerry Gold cheese and he was straight from Cork. But Mary Claire decided he was Italian and the name sounded good with Marie.

Now right here I want to explain about our names—the girls' names anyhow. I'm Ramona and my dark hair and name make some think I'm Spanish.

"Ah, it's the look of the Black Irish you have," they say.

I got my hair color from Jimmy O'Hara and I don't know whether he was Black Irish or not. But Mary Claire had this tradition of naming her daughters after whatever song she happened to humming around the time she went into labor.

I think she must have been coming off a bad patch—either getting over one man or falling in love with a new one—when I was born because *Ramona* was what was running through her head.

"*Ramona, I hear the mission bells above,*" she used to croon when she looked at me. "*Ra-moan-na, they're ringing out our song of love.*"

We all had the names of popular songs. There's my oldest sister Charmaine (*I'm lonely, my Charmaine, for you-ooo.*). Next, Georgia (*Georgia, Georgia, ... Just an old sweet song keeps Georgia on my mind.*) And finally the baby. Marie Dawn. (*Marie, the dawn is breaking ...*) Honestly! It made Marie so mad. And why Costello? Marie used to demand. By the time Marie was five years old, the rest of us couldn't even remember Costello's first name. Somebody thought it was Bobby until Charmaine remembered it was Buddy. We asked Mary Claire about it, but she couldn't remember either.

I never knew Jimmy O'Hara all that well. He drove a delivery truck for one on of the breweries, and I'd see him from time to time double parked in front of some bar or making a three-point turn. He was always nice to me though. Called me Cutie. He used to lean out the window of the cab and yell to me: "Hey, Cutie, howya doin'?" I don't think he remembered my name.

Everyone knew the Dargan girls and they kidded us about our names. We were just glad Mary Claire hadn't heard *Tangerine* on the radio when one of us was about to be born.

#

Horgan's and Lucky Elevens were the local watering holes and when Mary Claire fell off the wagon, she could be found in one place or the other, although Horgan's seemed to be the pub of choice. It was closer. When Eddie Horgan had determined that Mary Claire had exceeded her limit—and when even *he* had more integrity than to take another three bucks off her—he'd cut her off and instruct a runner to "Find a Dargan." Then one of us, having been found, would go down to Horgan's and try to persuade Mary Claire to come on home. I was usually the Dargan that the runner turned up because I was around the flat more often than the others due to my curious reading habit.

Mary Claire had a lovely singing voice, but we heard it mostly when she was in her cups.

"Ra-moan-*ah*," she'd warble as we were lurching home, "Ra-moooan-ah, I hear the mission bells..." This struck her as extremely funny. "Mission bells! St. *Brigid's* bells! Gate of ga-damn *Heaven's* bells! Hell's bells!" She'd laugh hysterically. Then she'd be singing again.

"Ra-*moan*-ah..."

Sometimes it took several Dargans to get Mary Clair home.

I got to know Horgan's pretty well. I certainly saw the inside of it often enough. And Eddie Horgan knew me. He hired me to wash glasses in the backroom before I was even legal.

Now you'd think, wouldn't you... like wouldn't you *think*... that my experience with Mary Claire would have made it plain to me that the drink didn't agree with a Dargan? Or in my case, an O'Hara or whoever I was? But no. Apparently not. And in the backroom at Horgan's I began my drinking career by tipping back a few when no one was looking.

I told myself I wasn't like Mary Claire. I never started singing and falling off barstools. No one had to send for another Dargan to bring me home.

Then one morning I woke up and my brother Mike was scowling at me.

"You don't remember last night, do you Ramona?"

"Wha?"

Mike was disgusted. Evidently I was establishing a little reputation as a chip off the old block. The old block being Mary Claire.

Horgan's and the Elevens were as familiar as our flat, but I didn't do much drinking in the pubs. Couldn't afford to. Back alleys and dark cars were where I learned about The Creature, and my tutors were older boys who were either willing to buy for me or willing to pick up the tab if I gave something back. And I gave what I had.

I dropped out of school in the eleventh grade and, needing money, enrolled in—what else?—bartending school. I put on make-up and high heels and lied about my age to get in. I knew how the bar scene worked and the money was good. Billy Hanley at the Lucky Elevens hired me. He should have known better.

I'll say this for myself though, I didn't drink on the job and I never pinched booze from Billy Hanley. Hardly ever. I was good at bartending. I knew how to pull a tap and how to pour a shot. I knew how to mix a drink too, although the call for mixed drinks in Southie was pretty limited. I was quick, cheerful, and pretty enough. I knew the regulars and knew how to chat them up. Knew who was safe to flirt with and who to stay cool of. A new customer would come into the Elevens and I had an instinct for how to give just the right amount of welcome and what to hold in reserve. Billy Hanley appreciated that. And I appreciated the regular paychecks. Much of which I drank after hours.

My brother Mike had to take me home more than once, I have to admit. And the other Dargans, Joe and Tommy and even Marie Dawn, had to handle drunk duty. I never sang though! Never once. But I picked a few fights with my siblings.

Finally they'd had enough. I think the rest of them had

some kind of Dargan meeting, and Char and Georgia did an intervention. They hauled me off to AA. Hauled me three or four times before I finally stood up and said. "My name is Ramona."

#

There is no such thing as a Boston accent. When someone talks about the Boston accent, you pretty much know they aren't from Boston. Or else they're tone deaf. Boston patois is as colorful and varied as a patchwork quilt, and it's comprised of a dozen or more local accents. The experienced linguist or someone with a good ear can position the speaker in Revere or in Lynn; there's a noticeable difference even though the towns are contiguous. Sometimes the speaker can even be identified by streets they've lived on. A South Shore accent is different from north-of-Boston speech. But Southie-speak is unique—different, even, from other South Shore accents.

I grew up speaking Southie. All us Dargan did. But I had Southie-speak trained out of me when I signed up for an elocution class at UMass. It was difficult. I practiced hard because I wanted to get past Southie, but my ear is still good, and I can still distinguish a D Street accent from one down City Point. And if I hang out with my brothers and sisters for longer than five minutes, I'm speaking Southie with the best of them.

For a couple years after I got sober, I continued to live with Mary Claire and whatever man or husband she was with at the time. The only other Dargan still "over home" was the youngest Marie Dawn. All the others were flung around the neighborhood or out beyond Southie. Charmaine, for instance, was all the way up in Billerica; Joe was down in Southboro, Georgia—she was the toney one—had crossed the Neponsett River to Milton, and finally even Marie Dawn moved on.

My routine was pretty rigid: AA meetings, classes at

UMass, and my job tending bar. Yes, that's right. There I am, going to AA in the afternoons and to the Armaugh at nights to tend bar. Now this is not condoned by AA, I can tell you that, but I needed tuition money and I stayed clean despite my environment. I mean I was around alcohol every single night and never touched a drop. You see, school meant everything to me. I earned my GPA after I'd gotten sober and I'd talked my way into UMass and my grades were good. I thought I was pretty much okay.

#

Mary Claire met her end beneath the wheels of a bus. You know that thing people are always saying? "What if so-and-so gets hit by a bus?" Well Mary Claire did. Right on Broadway. It didn't kill her—at least not right away—but it messed her up considerably. She hung between life and death at Boston Medical and meanwhile, all the Dargans hung out in the hallways, taking turns going in to see her. There were a lot of Dargans by then. In fact I was the only unmarried one, or I should say, never-married-one because Mike and Tommy were both divorced. These marriages had produced a lot of grandchildren for Mary Claire, but even the little Flynns and O'Hara's were known as Dargans. Go figure. Mary Claire's brother Danny McCarthy was hanging out with us too, and from all the nose-blowing and eye-wiping and general carrying on from him, you'd have thought he and his sister were the best of pals instead of a pair who'd been at each others' throats since they crawled out of the cradle.

Mary Claire eventually succumbed to her injuries. That's the way the newspapers and the medical establishment phrased it. Succumbed to her injuries. There was a funeral mass at St. Brigid's and then the Dargans came back to the flat to carry on in a wake. And to take what they wanted. Mementos, they said, of their mother. Their mother! None of us had every called

Mary Claire "Mother" for a single day of our lives!

Danny McCarthy had a jug of The Creature and everyone had a snort except for me and the little Flynns and Mike's kids. They talked about Mary Claire and about walking her home from Horgan's. They talked about her husbands and "husbands" and tried once again to remember the first name of Costello. They talked about Southie and how it had changed and how it wasn't the same now. Not as good. Then they all went away to the places they now called home.

I knew it was my turn to get out of Southie.

# # #

I'd finished up most of the classes I'd wanted to take at UMass anyway. I didn't graduate, but I'd never intended to. I just wanted to "better myself" as the old folks used to say. So I packed up what I had and moved north to start again.

I rented an apartment—not a flat, thank you, an apartment—in a North Shore town called Danvers. I stayed for there a while, and then moved several times. I found I could always get a job tending bar, and the jobs I found were in places that were more and more exclusive. Not joints. Not dives, but classy restaurants. A better class of customer came in, but the old skills I'd learned in Southie still applied. Move quickly, smile, look reasonably pretty, flirt just enough and don't chat up one customer too long. And don't speak Southie.

The Bowsprite was a newish restaurant built on the harbor. One whole wall is glass. The bar is about eighteen feet long and topped with copper, and the rest of it is wrapped in teak finished like a sailboat's hull. The eighteen-foot mirrored wall behind the bar is crammed with bottles of booze, exotic and priced to rival frankincense and myrrh, and a big copper samovar-thing for making espresso screams whenever there's an order for Irish coffee.

I loved the Bowsprite. I especially loved it late at night

when the last customers were lingering and I could wipe down the copper bar with a damp rag. The small TV up in the corner would be murmuring with late-night talk shows, and the folks at the bar, reluctant to leave and go out into the chilly night, had things to say. The sports talk and bicker about politics gave way then to the subjects of philosophy and art and sometimes religion. No voices got raised; just civilized conversation, and I'd feel warm and sheltered and calm.

And one night—early—into the Bowsprite came a man who turned out to be Dr. Stuart Hammer—a professor of ancient history at the small, North Shore liberal arts school called Talcott College. He ordered an ale, I remember, and sat quietly with it. And he'd wait for me to come along every so often and ask if I could get him anything more. He asked me about myself—my name and so forth. I told him Ramona but I didn't go beyond that. He sat there quite a while and finally I pointed out that his ale had gotten quite warm and couldn't I draw him a fresh one?

Well, he came back night after night and every time he'd ask me more about myself. Now, I know better than to get personal with the customers, so I'd feed him another bit of crap—little fictions, you knew—and go on down the bar tending to other customers, chatting up other folks, and Hammer's eyes would follow me the way a starving dog yearns after a platter of sizzling steak.

Well, you know how the story comes out: eventually I went out with Stuart Hammer and eventually he told me he was a widower and, weeping, he told me the sad story of Minnie Poole and he asked me to marry him. And I said to myself, "Oh, what the hell! He isn't bad looking. He's nice. He's well off. Why the hell not?"

I was getting tired of tending bar. Tired of the late nights and being on my feet all those hours. That big mausoleum in

Ipswich was looking pretty good. I decided to retire.

# # #

Chapter 23

"Wicked cool!" Ramona O'Hara shifted into Southie-speak when she'd finished reading Nell's draft of her story.

"Did I get most of the details right?" Nell asked anxiously. "Did I capture your voice?"

"Now you're sounding like Ann Fitzmaurice," Ramona told her, "you know, wanting to catch a likeness. And yes, I think you did. The only way I can tell though is because it sounds comfortable. Familiar."

"Whew," said Nell.

"And by the way," Ramona continued, "I think Ann *has* captured a likeness. I think the portrait looks just like me— well, maybe a tad more glamorous—and I can't understand what Stuart is carrying on about."

Nell nodded but proceeded carefully.

"Perhaps his view of you is considerably different from the way the rest of us see you. Or from the way your mirror sees you. I guess we can't exactly know what he sees."

"He's frustrated the stuffing out of Ann though," Ramona

observed. "She's ready to bite the bristles off of her brushes."

"Have you see her lately?" Nell wanted to know. "Are you still doing sittings?"

"At this point, no. Ann says its just details and she can do the finishing without me."

Ramona handed back the typed draft. Nell shivered.

"I'm glad to have your approval on this," she said. "but the tough part is still to come. I've got to show this to Stuart."

Nell made a wry face.

"I'm pretty sure he'll notice things that he did not share with me. And I have to tell you, Ramona, that this is very different from the story Stuart told me."

Ramona's smile was extraordinary.

"I know!" she said, "Isn't it a hoot? Stuart sees things in his own way. The world according to Stuart."

Nell began to wonder if Hammer had also dreamed up— or doctored up—the story of Minnie the Has-Bean heiress. She began to wonder if Minnie's fall down the stairs had happened as simply and accidentally as Hammer had described. What, indeed, did the world according to Stuart look like?

"There are things that I've simply never shared with Stuart," Ramona said. She smiled enigmatically.

Nell's eyebrows went up.

"Stuart," Ramona continued, "knows what he wants to know, hears what he wants to hear and when he doesn't want to know or hear something, he simply doesn't accept them. I gave up long ago trying to pierce the veil."

"What do you think he'll say?" Nell asked. "Or do?"

Ramona shrugged. "No clue."

"Only one way to find out then," Nell said grimly. "Show 'im."

Chapter 24

Stuart Hammer frowned. With a dismissive flip, he tossed the manuscript onto the desk where it landed with a small splat. He removed his reading glasses and pinched the bridge of his nose. He closed his eyes. Nell maintained her silence—maintained it with some difficulty. Then Hammer opened his eyes.

"You write very well, Mrs. Bane, but I can't imagine *who* you are writing *about*."

He was speaking to her the way he might speak to a student—a very dim student—who had turned in a disappointing paper.

"Have you actually read the draft, Stuart?"

It seemed to Nell that Hammer had merely glanced through it. Moreover, she found his tone insulting.

"I read enough," he answered. "And I didn't like what I read. I don't recall, Mrs. Bane, furnishing you with many—indeed most—of the details you've seen fit to stuff into this...this piece of *fiction*."

Ah, the condescending professororial tone was continuing. Nell was damned though, if she would accept a defensive position.

"It is my job as a writer" she replied calmly, "to supply color and action to a written piece. Indeed, that is essential. And so I did some research on my own and yes, where detail and color were lacking..." and here Nell fixed Hammer with a penetrating gaze of her own and added ..."I supplied them."

Several moments passed as they sat there in a face-off. Client and writer. Bully and subject . Silence was rigid between them. The first one to speak loses, Nell reminded herself. So she was pleased when Stuart Hammer was the one to break the silence.

"Perhaps you are right about one thing," he acknowledged. "I haven't really read the manuscript through and I may have rushed to some conclusions. So I'll grant you this. I will give careful attention to the draft. See if I can recognize Ramona in any of it. And then we'll be in touch to discuss the project further. I take it that is alright with you?"

Nell inclined her head in a gracious nod.

"It is, Stuart. And I am pleased you see it this way. I'll wait your call, then?"

"You may do so," he replied stiffly.

My goodness, Nell thought, how formal we've become. She stood up.

"I'll take my leave then," she said.

"And I," Stuart Hammer replied, rising also, "will see you to the stairs."

They walked in silence down the corridor. Nell was conscious of their footsteps which seemed inordinately loud in the empty hall. She paused at the top of the stairs.

"I'll wait for your call then," she summarized, reaching for the railing.

"Yes indeed," he replied.

Then suddenly he lurched into her. More of shove really. For a microsecond, Nell saw the long run of stairs beneath her, but she grabbed the railing and caught herself somehow. She whirled to aim an accusatory glare at Hammer.

"Oh! Beg your pardon," he said, "Lost my balance there."

He smirked a mock apology.

Nell was incredulous. She continued to stare at him but Stuart Hammer just blandly gazed at her, smiling a small, strange smile.

Nell turned slowly and continued carefully down the stairs, holding the railing as she descended. When she reached the bottom, she turned once again, this time to look up. He was still standing there. Watching her. Nell didn't speak, just turned away and walked up the corridor, restraining herself from hurrying and forcing herself to walk slowly, heading for the dim light that shone through the glass in the door ahead.

Inside her head, something almost audible said: "Minnie Poole."

Chapter 25

Nell hit her mental refresh button over and over, and every time she replayed the scene on the stairs with Stuart Hammer, the event grew more improbable. More impossible to believe. She began to doubt her sanity. Perhaps he really had lost his balance. Perhaps—worse of all—perhaps the whole incident was a figment of her warped, over-active writer's imagination!

Moreover, the compromise she'd agreed to with Stuart Hammer cast her in a passive position. She'd made a mistake. She had agreed to do nothing until he called her—until *he* had read the manuscript and decided to react to it. Hammer had suggested—and she'd agreed—that he would call when he'd read it and wanted to arrange a meeting. Until then, she would have to wait and twiddle her thumbs. She should have given him a deadline, but instead she had given him the upper hand. Oh well, nothing she could do about that now.

So the days turned over and became a week, then two weeks. And the waiting game continued.

And it was a game! Nell was convinced of this! It was a

little technique devised by Stuart Hammer to confuse her, frustrate her, wear her down and make her vulnerable. Make her more pliable to his manipulations.

"The dirty little rat," Nell said to herself. "And I enabled him! I actually agreed to his terms and now all the power is on his end."

And she was disgusted with herself.

Another day passed. Then another.

"I've got to get out of here!" Nell said.

But all her friends seemed busy. She called them, one by one to propose a road trip to Maine, to the Cape, to Vermont, but each friend offered a regretful excuse. Bunty had a deadline for some pottery. Ann Fitzmaurice was entertaining her sister-in-law from Arizona. Robert Hutchins had a client who was requiring his complete attention, and Jerry Gasso, of course, was happily up to his collarbone in fabrics and color wheels. Even Nell's old friend Madeline Kaiser, who could usually be counted on for adventure, was bogged down for it was finals time at the end of the Taft University term, and there were test to prepare and term papers to grade.

"Very well," said the Little Red Hen (a.k.a. Nell Bane), "I'll go by myself." And she did.

But the impromptu trip to Portland for a prowl through the shops on the waterfront and a lunch in one of the delightful restaurants along Fore Street was a dud. No one to talk with. No one to gasp appreciatively when she pointed out the eagle drifting over the treetops as they drove or the doe poised beside the road. Luckily it didn't dart into the path of her car.

And in the end, the Little Red Hen returned to Newburyport and turned her kitchen over to the making of soup. An unusual recipe had been nibbling at her curiosity and she finally gave way to it, deciding she wouldn't admit to any of her friends that she was actually making peanut butter pumpkin soup.

PEANUT BUTTER PUMPKIN SOUP
2 T unsalted butter
1 15-oz can of pumpkin
1 medium sweet potato (about 1 cup), cooked and pureed
1/2 cup organic peanut butter, smooth or crunchy
3 cups chicken stock
1/2 tsp freshly ground black pepper
1/2 tsp salt
Snipped chives and sour cream for garnish
Nell melted the butter in a saucepan and stirred in the pumpkin, sweet potato and peanut butter. She added the stock, salt and pepper and simmered the soup for 20 minutes.

But the cooking and prep times, added together, amounted to less than forty-five minutes, and that included the cooking and pureeing of the sweet potato. And while the soup was good—creamy and flavorful—it had failed to absorb Nell's interest for much more than an hour. Meanwhile, Stuart Hammer still had the upper hand.

Chapter 26

With Bunty in the passenger's seat, Nell shot out Water Street at the crest of the speed limit. Which was a blazing thirty-miles per hour. Ann Fitzmaurice had sent up an SOS. Stuart Hammer had seen—and rejected—the finished portrait of Ramona O'Hara, and Ann was veering dangerously between fury and deep purple depression.

They found Ann in the kitchen, slamming pot lids into a drawer beneath the stove. She was wearing her besmirched artist's apron though, and she looked up, scowling furiously, when they walked in.

"Uh-oh," said Bunty, looking at Nell, "Maybe we'd better turn right around and walk out. It doesn't look safe in here."

"No, no, no," Ann Fitzmaurice said hastily, "I'm sorry, it's just that I'm livid! I'm so mad at that man I could bite through my own paintbrush. I could...*ooh!*"

She bounced to her feet.

"Look!" she commanded, indicating the studio.

Obediently Nell and Bunty swiveled to follow the direction

of her pointing hand.

"Well, no," Ann said sensibly. "Not from here. You can't see from here! Go in and take a look at the easel. Tell me what you see."

Uneasily, Nell and Bunty jostled into the studio area and stood in front of the canvas in the poses of sensitive art critics at an exhibition—critics who weren't exactly sure what they were expected to see. Or say. Ann came right along with them.

"Well?" she demanded.

"I see a painting," Bunty said tentatively, obviously taking the most general tack. "Of a woman," she added helpfully.

"It's Ramona," Nell said decisively. "There's no mistaking. You've caught a perfect likeness, Ann, and what's more, you've managed to capture her amazing vitality. You've painted her energy. I can't imagine how you've done that. Or, for that matter, what more you could have done."

"Well, of course, I've never seen Ramona." Bunty came to her own defense. "I've no idea what she looks like in person, but I would certainly say this is a very fine painting. Professional quality."

Ann Fitzmaurice was beginning to look slightly mollified.

"Good," she said. "I thought maybe I was crazy. Franklin has been telling me all along that it's fine, but I was losing confidence in myself."

She shook her head.

"These past few weeks have been horrible," she continued. "I feel like I can't do anything correctly. I've even thought of giving up painting."

"Don't think that!" Nell was fierce. "That's what he wants you to think, Stuart Hammer."

She shook her head and discovered to her surprise that both hands were balled into tight fists.

"Listen, I'll tell you what happened to *me*. What he did to me. Any chance you'd make us a cup of tea, Ann?"

Ann Fitzmaurice was quick to move to the kitchen and fill the kettle, but she didn't want to wait for the water to boil and the tea to steep. She wanted the story right away.

"Tell!" she demanded.

And so Nell told about her meeting in Stuart's office. She described Stuart's reaction to the manuscript, the words they'd exchanged and finally, the compromise they'd reached that Stuart would read and consider the draft, then call her and they'd meet again.

"But that was weeks ago," Nell said, aggrieved, "Well, a couple weeks anyhow, and I haven't heard Word One from him. But this is the interesting part..."

And she described the incident on the stairs.

"He actually shoved me," she said. "Took his shoulder and gave an intentional bump into my upper arm. And hard! I grabbed the railing just in time, but the blow all but knocked me off my pins and down the stairway."

Ann was staring at her in horror. Bunty Whitney looked angry.

"And you said he was harmless!" she accused. "Robert told you to be careful and you insisted he was just a dotty, harmless Western Civ professor."

Nell nodded sheepishly.

Bunty's anger blew away in an instant though. Nell was accustomed to seeing this, and wasn't surprised when her friend's face smoothed into the neutral mask of the psychotherapist.

"Is that tea ready, Ann? Good." Bunty accepted her cup.

"Now. What we're dealing with here, I think, is clearly a passive aggressive personality."

She stopped and looked at first Nell then at Ann with her eyebrows raised, inviting comment. When each had nodded,

Bunty continued. "Do you understand what that means and the implications it can have for the people involved?"

"In a general way, I think I do," Nell said, "but perhaps you can provide some detail."

"Passive aggressive individuals—appearances often to the contrary—are hostile individuals," Bunty said. "They will often appear very mild and pleasant, but that's because they have difficulty expressing their anger openly. They wouldn't want you to think poorly of them by displaying common forms of anger, so they have developed indirect means to express their fury."

Bunty paused and looked sharply at Ann and Nell.

"Is this making sense?"

Both nodded emphatically.

"Yes, go on," said Ann. She looked quite avid, Nell thought.

"Passive aggression," continued Bunty, "is a form of covert abuse—sometimes so masked or subtle that the victim doesn't even recognize that she or he has been a victim. Here's an example. Say someone hauls off and slugs you in the mouth. Well, the abuse is obvious, isn't it? It was intentional. But covert abuse is veiled; sometimes the action even seems loving. Stuart Hammer shoved you, Nell. Possibly even meant to bump you off balance and send you careening down those stairs. But he masked his physical aggression by shoving you with his *shoulder*, then apologizing and smiling innocently. But he *intended* to shove you on the stairs, and if you'd tumbled down then, well too bad, but it was your fault. *You* were the one who lost your balance. He didn't want you to think he pushed you on purpose though, hence the little-boy-innocent smirk. Some victims would have been taken in by his guile. And although you weren't, you did begin to wonder if you'd been mistaken by thinking his action was deliberate, right?"

Nell could see Bunty's point and she nodded agreement.

"He seems very loving to his wife though," Ann pointed out. "In fact he adores her. He willingly agreed to pay a handsome sum to have her portrait painted. I never saw any signs of passive aggressive behavior connected with Ramona O'Hara."

"Ah," said Bunty. "You think not? Then consider this. The passive aggressive individual often—not always, but often—has some relationship issues and some reality issues. They typically write their own reality."

She gave Ann a meaningful look.

"Didn't you experience this when Stuart Hammer looked at the portrait you were painting? You knew, didn't you, that you had achieved a good likeness of Ramona, but apparently your reality didn't match Stuart's."

Ann's eyes widened.

"The passive aggressive individual *objectifies* the object of affection. The only value that 'object' has is to feed his emotional need. I doubt Stuart sees Ramona as an actual person—one with feelings and needs of her own. To Stuart, she is merely an object, like his car, for example, and he cares for her the way he'd fastidiously care for his car. It's a possession—an extension of himself, you see."

"And to us," murmured Nell, "that looks like love and adoration."

Bunty nodded. "Adoration it is. Love—I don't think so. Although Stuart Hammer probably would. I doubt he knows the difference."

She placed her empty teacup on the table with a smart smack.

"I'm decommissioning my shingle," she declared. "Enough psycho-babble! I'll merely say that Stuart Hammer appears to be hanging on some very loose hinges."

"Well, I know what I intend to do," Ann Fitzmaurice told

them. "I am declaring this portrait finished! And I am going to send my invoice to Stuart Hammer tomorrow!"

Chapter 27

"I'm playing a waiting game, Robert," Nell told her old friend. "And I'm tired of sitting around twiddling my thumbs. Can I entice you out to lunch?"

"As it happens," Robert Hutchins said, "my work load has eased considerably, and I can think of nothing more charming than to go to lunch with you."

And so they agreed to meet once again at the Black Cow in Newburyport, and Nell looked forward to a pleasant lunch in the "ship's cabin" booth. The glasses of wine they had ordered arrived, and Nell lifted her glass then set it down again, making a design on the table with the wet circles the glass imprinted, and she considered, while she did this, whether to tell Robert about Stuart Hammer and the stair incident. Robert watched her.

"What's on your mind?" he asked quietly.

Nell looked up quickly.

Robert laughed. "No need to look so innocent. I know when something's brewing in your brain."

Nell let her shoulders sag as she sighed.

"I don't know if it's a good thing or a bad thing to be so transparent. Or maybe you're just psychic."

"Maybe," agreed Robert, waiting.

"You'll just say 'I told you so,'" Nell said.

"Maybe. But what if I promise not to say it?"

"Okay. Let's see if you can control yourself."

And Nell repeated—this time to Robert Hutchins—the incident she'd described to Bunty and Ann.

To his credit, Robert didn't claim that he'd warned her, but one corner of his mouth tucked in and he put on an expression of distaste.

"I know, I know," Nell moaned.

"More to the point," said Robert, "what are we going to do about it?"

"We? I you mean. Well..." Nell thought for a few moments, conscious of Robert's intent gaze. "Well... I'm going to be more careful. Watch my step...." Her voice trailed off.

"You should certainly watch your step, but Hammer may not try that specific trick again. He may try something else though I can't even suggest what. But you are so innocent Nell. So quick to believe the best of everyone, and you can be blind sometimes to people's faults."

"I can only be what I am," she protested humbly.

"True. But you *can* be careful."

Her wet glass design had dried up. She tried imprinting a new circle with the base of her glass but there was no effect.

Robert Hutchins relented.

"Time to order, I think," he said kindly. "Now let me bring you up to date on Jerry's great project."

Chapter 28

Nell's waiting game continued, and her frustration mounted. She held interior debates about initiating contact with Stuart Hammer. She rehearsed imaginary excuses for calling. ("Oh hi Stuart, I was just thinking about you..." "Funny thing, Stuart, but I can't remember how we left things. Was I going to call you? Or were you going to call me? *Heh-heh.*"). But in the end she did nothing. To call Stuart Hammer would simply be another form of the first-one-to-speak-loses game. She was not going to grovel.

And then he did call, catching her completely off-guard.

"I've read your draft," he said. There was no inflection in his voice. Nell could read no emotion in it. She was forced, however, to speak.

"Yes?" she said, "And...?"

"I have some reactions, naturally. Quite a few in fact, and I'd like to see you."

And so Nell and Stuart Hammer agreed to meet once more in his office, this time to discuss the manuscript in detail.

They'd tussled a bit about the meeting time. Nell was determined that the meeting should take place in the middle of the day when the history department would be busy with students coming and going and with teaching assistants and professors chatting in the hall, conducting meetings and operating the department's copy machines. Stuart had pointed out that he was generally busy at those times—student conferences and so forth—and insisted that after-hours would be preferable. But Nell held her ground. The meeting would be mid-day or not at all.

Stuart Hammer did not rise from his desk chair when Nell entered the office, rapping on the doorjamb to announce her arrival. This minor breach of manners was not lost on Nell.

Hammer was all business. He turned to a deep pile of papers on the side of his desk and pretended to have difficulty locating the manuscript among all his *important* material.

He's trivializing, Nell told herself. She smiled inwardly, thinking Bunty would be proud of her to notice this. She sat with perfect composure, her hands loosely folded in her lap.

"Ah! Here we are."

As proof, Stuart held the manuscript in the air, flapping it slightly. He placed it exactly in front of him and put on his reading glasses. "Ah," he repeated, looking as if it were an long-lost but slightly unfamiliar object now suddenly seen again, "Now then...ah, Mrs. Bane..."

And Nell saw that she'd been returned to the role of failing student, the role of supplicant sitting meekly at the side of the professor's desk.

"As you requested, I read your manuscript carefully, Mrs. Bane. Read through it several times, in fact, and your 'facts' are very suspect. I can't imagine where you found them or dreamed them up. Your writing style is adequate but the material is so badly flawed that I cannot accept it. It's completely unacceptable. Now if you want to revise this and resubmit it, I will try to make the time to read it again."

Hammer pulled off his reading glasses and regarded her with an expression that was obviously intended to appear kind.

"I encourage you to keep trying, Nell," he continued with false benevolence. "I am confident you can create the word portrait of Ramona that she deserves and that I desire."

He held the manuscript out to her.

Nell had no intention of taking it. To do so, would let Stuart Hammer completely off the hook. She shook her head.

"There's no need," she said. "I have the draft on my computer, and if any changes needed to be made, I could easily do it. But frankly, Stuart, I don't see the need for further work. I believe I have fulfilled the task you described. You see, I have a confession to make. Needing more resource material than you provided, I contacted Ramona O'Hara and interviewed her quite extensively. She corrected a number of misperceptions I had—details I received from you. She is quite adamant that her story be accurate. Admittedly, hers is a gritty story and it's a far cry from the fairy tale you spun out to me—but it is hers. Her story. And I've written it the way she wants it to be told. She wants it to be true."

As Nell made this speech, Stuart Hammer's face, had undergone a several changes of color and expression. When she finished, his face was purple—had turned from white to purple. His mouth, it had been opening and closing like a fish's, was now set in a grim line.

"I don't want to hear any more of this!" he snapped. "Ramona isn't...well, she isn't always aware of what she's saying. Yes, that's it! She isn't aware. What you've taken as gospel, Mrs. Bane, isn't the truth. I know the truth. Now I don't intend to hear anymore of this!"

And Hammer tried to dismiss her with a gesture toward the open door of his office. Nell continued to stare at him, but he had lowered his head and was pretending with all his might to read a document on his desk. Nell, looking down, saw he was reading it upside down. She rose with a sigh.

"I'm sorry it had to come to this," she said softly. "I'll be in touch, Stuart."

The hall of the history department was busy with people hurrying to classrooms or running errands, so Nell could walk to the staircase with an assurance of safety. She was relieved to let the heavy door of Burton Hall close behind her. She trotted down the granite steps but at the bottom, compelled by the feeling of eyes upon her—boring into her—she turned and gazed upward. It took her several seconds to locate the second floor window where a figure stood. It was Stuart Hammer. Their eyes locked. Nell was determined not to look away and eventually Hammer, with a sneer of disgust, spun away from the window.

The spell was shattered. Nell was released. She hurried toward her car.

Chapter 29

Nell was disturbed. She couldn't seem to shake an uneasy feeling—a feeling that someone or something was following her. Stuart's gaze from the window's height seemed all-seeing, powerful enough to follow her car even as she drove home. And his image didn't leave her on the highway. It stayed with her, sending shivers in spasms along her spine. It refused to release its grip even when she tried concentrating on something else. She tried remembering the lyrics to Cole Porter songs and tried naming the capitals of all the states on the Eastern seaboard. She recited the Gettysburg Address but nothing seemed to exorcise the specter of Stuart Hammer.

For the rest of the afternoon she was haunted by Hammer's fetch—a spectral double of the living man. An entity conjured out of Irish folklore. A wraith risen from black bog of Caraugh Duh itself.

The manuscript on Stuart's desk joined the haunting. Two very different stories. She had tried blending them but the basic properties were so different that the elements seemed to repel each other. Like oil and water, the stories kept separating into individual accounts.

Nell had been half afraid that Ramona's real story would shatter Stuart's thrall. Afraid that once he knew the truth—knew that the object of his adoration wasn't who he thought—the enchantment might break. And of course, she, Nell, would be responsible, and therefore responsible as well for whatever happened next.

As it happened though, Stuart Hammer had simply rejected the truth. He could do that, she now understood, by simply projecting responsibility for the story directly onto Nell and accusing her of lying.

"A real case of shoot the messenger," she murmured. "Oh well," she told herself consolingly, "perhaps its better than he's mad at me rather than at Ramona. I have more places to hide than she does."

But the meeting in Stuart's office continued to nibble at her. She had felt anger radiating from some hot, molten core inside him, and she remembered Bunty saying: "The passive aggressive personality doesn't deal well with anger. He may not be able to express it acceptably, and if forced to deal with a problem, will withdraw from the situation or the relationship—that is, withdraw from you."

Bunty's phrases came rocketing back: "The passive aggressive will deny evidence of wrong-doing ... will distort or refute what you know to be real ... will organize facts to construct a version of reality that seems to him, more logical."

"I'm going to make soup!" Nell declared.

MEATBALL TORTELINI SOUP
1 sweet onion, chopped
2 medium carrots quartered lengthwise and sliced
1 T olive oil

32-ounces of chicken stock
1/2 cup water
1 pound of small meatballs, either homemade or purchased one 9-ounce packed of refrigerated cheese tortellini
4 cups fresh spinach, chopped or torn
3 T bottled red roasted red peppers, chopped (optional)
1 T lemon juice
Italian seasonings of choice

In a Dutch oven, sauté the onion and carrots until tender. Add the stock and water and bring to a boil. Add the tortellini and meatballs (thaw the meatballs in the microwave if they are frozen). Simmer the soup until the pasta is tender. Stir in the spinach, red pepper, and lemon juice and simmer 3 minutes more. Adjust the seasonings.

Soup-making was a place where she could lose herself. When the vapors of simmering soup began to rise, her head could clear.

But the therapeutic result of soup making was temporary. That night Nell tossed in bed, twisting the sheets to ropes as she dreamed of pale kings and princes riding gaunt horses. Lines of *La Belle Dame sans Merci* repeated nauseatingly through her dreams. The ghastly statue on Boston Common— the one she'd always associated with pale kings and princes, *death pale were they all*—galloped down from its plinth beside Charles Street and the riders hurled lines at her as they rode.

I met a lady o'er the mead, full beautiful, a faery's child...

And then Ramona O'Hara swirled past, laughing maniacally and tossing her black hair.

her hair was long, her foot was light and her eyes were wild...

Nell thrashed and twisted. She thought she was awake and at the same time knew she wasn't. And in the morning she was feverish and exhausted.

In the kitchen, in early morning's cold light, she made tea and her hands shook. She'd not known dreams could have such a debilitating effect but after a half hour, she knew it was more than the dreams—she knew she had a case of flu.

Chapter 30

"Ramona," Nell said frankly, as soon as Ramona's musical "Hi there" greeted her call. "I am stuck, to tell you the truth. I gave the word portrait manuscript to Stuart, and I don't know where to go from here. I'm wondering if we can get together and piece out a few things I don't understand."

"I don't see why not," Ramona O'Hara said reasonably. "Would you like to see the mansion?"

Nell was surprised.

"Well, yes, I would like that very much, but Stuart..." she trailed off delicately.

"Come on a Tuesday," Ramona said. "He's always busy at school on Tuesdays because he has an early class and a late one and in between he schedules student conferences. It'll be fine, and I'd love to show you around."

So Nell was following—or trying to follow—the directions Ramona had given her.

"You can't miss it." That's what Ramona had said.

This statement, in Nell's opinion, always sounded the

Doomsday knell of her chances of getting anywhere easily. It was right up there with: "It's very simple."

"It is never simple," Nell grumbled, glancing down at the handwritten directions on the seat beside her, "and I *can* miss it. And I usually do."

The road forked and Nell checked her instructions. Ramona hadn't mentioned a fork.

"So it's fifty-fifty," Nell said and pulled the wheel to the left. But she'd guessed correctly and within a few yards the spread that Ramona had described opened up on the passenger's side. There indeed was the wide, flat meadow, shorn now for the winter, and along one side, stretched the straight drive—almost a road really—lined with mature sycamore trees and running all the way to the house. And Nell had her first look at the Has-Bean Mansion.

Nell was interested in architecture, but the Has-Bean place fit no style she could identify. Inclusive, was the best description she could manage. And that was being charitable. The architect had evidently borrowed from every form known to civilization and had hashed it all together into an impressively muddled structure. At least it was large.

"It's great to have company," Ramona said happily when she opened the door, "we so rarely do. Come on in."

Nell did, looking around as she came. The impression she'd received on the outside carried to the inside.

"Give it A-plus for consistency," she thought.

Ramona was eager to show Nell around. An imposing staircase, more appropriate to New Orleans than Ipswich, Massachusetts, rose out of the entrance hall and scaled the heights of the house. Looking up, Nell wondered if these were the stairs down which Minnie Poole, the late Has-Bean heiress, had plunged. She hadn't the nerve to ask.

In the living room, however, she encountered Minnie

Poole. Or her facsimile. There was the photograph Ramona had described, blown to a great size and hand-tinted by an artist who'd had a heavy hand and a taste for strong color. The Has-Bean heiress, Nell decided was very much as Ramona had said. Not pretty, nor even handsome, but despite the awful tinting, she still looked jolly and approachable. Moreover, there was a kindliness and good humor in her face that drew Nell's instant affection as well as her sympathy. Ramona had described Minnie as a sizey lady, and Nell saw she was indeed several years older and several sizes larger than her dapper little husband. Ramona and Nell stood side by side and regarded the portrait together.

"Well, it's bright," Nell said helpfully.

"Yup," agreed Ramona O'Hara.

Standing side by side, they silently contemplated the portrait of the late Has-Bean heiress.

Nell looked around the room. Like Minnie herself, the room was sizey, but its size had just allowed it to accept more than its share of stuff. Furnishings from the 'twenties, 'thirties, 'forties and 'fifties were well represented. Cabinets and consoles, rockers and ottomans, a grand piano and three sofas, two of which wore crocheted afgans, were crammed into the room. In a corner, Nell spotted an old cabinet television set from the era of TV's adolescence.

Apparently Stuart Hammer had been content to move into this time capsule and exist there happily. But how had Ramona maintained her sanity amid all that cabbage rose wallpaper and those flower-printed draperies?

Nell had to ask.

Ramona O'Hara laughed.

"I know what you mean. But Stuart is very protective of the stuff here. He feels it should all be preserved, and he has not allowed me to change a thing."

"I suppose it could have something to do with his chosen profession," Nell said. "Ancient civilization and history and all." She was trying to be charitable. "But how do you stand it?"

Ramona shrugged.

"It just seemed easier to leave it all alone rather than rock Stuart's little boat. He doesn't react well to changes in his cages. And frankly, I wouldn't know how to begin," she continued. "Nothing in my background prepared me to take on interior decorating of this scope. I grew up in a series of flats in the Southie projects, remember."

She strolled out of the living room with Nell following.

"However..." she continued, talking as she went, "Stuart did allow me my own room. My little suite, I call it. Come."

Nell followed Ramona through the house until they arrived at a small room at the back of the house—a room that may have once been a three-season porch that had been winterized and deeded to Ramona.

Saturated color—the shade of boiled shrimp—vibrated from the walls, and here the furniture was quite contemporary with Lucite tables and a hard-looking sofa that was about as inviting as a bus station bench.

But here, on this upholstered bench, Nell sat. Or tried to sit. Scrounging back into the sofa, she discovered her legs were sticking straight out in front like the legs of a small child trying out an adult's chair. Looking around, she snagged a throw pillow and stuffed it behind her back. Once the pillow had boosted her forward and she was able to bend her knees over the sofa's edge, she was considerably more comfortable. She smiled at Ramona who was watching her expectantly.

"Before I bring you up-to-date on the word portrait project, I should ask how you are coming along with Tenderly."

"Everything's fine," Ramona said. "Things are coming

along just fine."

She smiled.

Nell, watching the smile and reading Ramona's body language, got an odd sense of ... well, something. But clearly Ramona didn't want to discuss it, so Nell shifted the subject.

"Well. The word portrait. As I told you on the phone, I gave the draft you'd approved to Stuart." Nell was blunt. "He didn't like it."

Ramona's expression didn't change

"I didn't think he would," she said.

Nell cleared her throat, "The thing is, he seemed very surprised by some of the—well, revelations. He demanded to know where I'd gotten those details, and he accused me of promulgating lies about you. He said the facts were absolutely untrue."

She was watching Ramona carefully to gauge some reaction but could read none.

"So I am in a state of some confusion," she continued after a pause. "Right now, I've begun to think that one of you is having me on, as you Irish say. I've become unsure of which of you is telling the truth."

Several seconds passed before Ramona spoke. Her expression, however never changed. She continued to regard Nell pleasantly, the way you'd encourage a shy child who is trying very hard to express herself or recite something memorized for a performance

"Both," she said.

"Both? You're both telling the truth? Care to explain that?"

Ramona relented. She sat back against the cushions of her chair and sighed softly.

"Okay, I guess it's this way. Stuart never knew my whole story. Not really. Not at first. Then later, when I tried to tell him, he didn't want to hear it. I told him—kept trying to tell him—but he couldn't handle it."

Nell, watching Ramona intently, was silent.

Ramona appeared to be organizing her story.

"When Stuart started coming to the Bowsprite to sit at the bar and hold that glass of warm ale, I realized that he wasn't coming in for the ale. He was coming in to watch me. To talk to me.

"His patter wasn't very original or interesting. 'What's your name?' he'd ask. 'Where are you from?' A bartender gets to know just how much personal information to share. You've gotta protect yourself you know, so you edit. So I told him my name and then the 'facts' I'd give out got a little blurry.

"'O'Hara', he say. 'You're Irish?' Well, yeah. Then he talked about my pretty, black hair ('Black Irish?' Yeah) and my Spanish name, hence the Spanish Armada and so on and so forth. So Stuart Hammer sat there on that barstool, weaving my story out of the conversational bits I'd drop casually and mostly out of his own imagination, and eventually he invented a whole, romantic history that he hung on me like...I dunno...like a mink coat or something."

Ramona paused in thought. It appeared to Nell that she had traveled back in time and for the first time in a long time was reviewing the way they'd come.

"He had made up this whole story out of bits I'd told him. Made a whole patchwork quilt out of scraps. And I just let him go on assuming it all was true simply because it was easier. It was easier not to correct his assumptions. So I'd just let the facts slide."

"Tacit agreement," Nell supplied.

"Yeah. Anyhow, I could see it pleased Stuart to see me as this romantic woman of mystery with a glamorous past. What harm could it do, I thought, to make a lonely man happy? What harm could it do to spin little inventions that caught his imagination and pleased him? I had no idea that Stuart Hammer would become more than a customer mooning like a sick cat at the end of the bar. I didn't know much about him, really, and then, before I knew what was happening, I was being taken out to dinner in fancy restaurants. I was opening gifts of expensive jewelry, receiving bouquets of flowers. My gosh, the only flowers I'd ever gotten were half-dead ones I bought for myself off a street vendor in Downtown Crossing or off a kiosk on the platform in North Station."

Ramona O'Hara's attention had shifted. She was gazing out the window but whatever she was seeing wasn't outside—it was somewhere in the past.

"When he asked me to marry him, it was very sudden. There was no, you know, lead-up to the proposal, it was just—*bam!*—and the deal was on the table. And my answer was just as sudden. 'Yes,' I said, 'Yes, I will'. And later I thought oh my, what have I done? But then it was too late. I couldn't go back on my word."

Now Ramona turned her full gaze on Nell.

"And here I am," she said. With a laugh, she turned her palms out to indicate the room where they were sitting. "Here! In Ipswich. In the house that Minnie Poole's father built."

Nell took a deep breath and asked the question.

"Are you happy here? Here in the house that Minnie Poole's father built? Here with Stuart Hammer?"

Ramona actually laughed.

"Happy? I never thought about it. I have no idea!"

Nell sat quietly, regarding Ramona. She had one more question.

"If Stuart knew the truth—knew it from you in your words, what do you think would happen?"

A shrug. "No idea."

"If Stuart knew the real story, do you think he would harm

you, Ramona? Has Stuart every tried to harm you?"

"Stuart?" Ramona O'Hara was incredulous. "I don't think he'd even step on an ant."

Chapter 31

"I've made up my mind," said Ann Fitzmaurice. "I'm not going to jump through Stuart Hammer's hoops any longer. He will never be satisfied! He can't even tell me what he doesn't like about Ramona's portrait. 'I'll know it when I see it,' he says. Well, that'll never happen. We could go on for years with him waiting to 'see it'."

Nell glanced toward Ann's studio and was surprised to see a smaller canvas installed on the easel. The portrait of Ramona O'Hara leaned against a wall in the dimmest corner of the room.

"Are you going to tell him to come and get the painting?" she asked.

"No. I'm going to send my invoice. When he pays it—pays it in full—he can have the portrait. If he wants it, he'll have to come with a check in his hand."

Nell rather envied Ann her decision. She had taken a stand.

"But what if he doesn't come?"

Ann shrugged.

"Then he doesn't come. And he doesn't get the portrait, obviously. But I don't know...I have a funny hunch he won't be able to turn his back on the painting. It would be like abandoning something that's his. Like abandoning your child."

Nell, thinking this over, nodded.

"Given who he is, I think you may be right."

Nell scratched her ear.

"I'm in a similar situation," she said wistfully. "He tried to give the manuscript back to me to 'work on' and I wouldn't take it. It seemed I'd be playing right into the hands of a passive aggressive if I did that."

She wondered if she should follow Ann's example and send Hammer a demand for payment.

"He paid the first third of our arrangement," she said, "and he still owes the remaining two-thirds, the final third of which is due upon delivery of the manuscript. Trouble is, he won't *take* delivery. He can always claim the project isn't finished to his liking."

Nell had, of course, told Ann that Ramona's story was different from Stuart's account.

"Was he surprised?" Ann asked now. "Shocked when he read her version?"

"He didn't appear to believe me," Nell told her. "Accused me of lying. Of making it all up."

"Well, she's his adored wife," Ann said sourly. "Who's he going to believe? You? Or the object of his affection? You lose, chum."

"I don't care about winning or losing," Nell said. "I just want to be paid."

Chapter 32

Nell Bane and Ann Fitzmaurice made a pact. They would prepare final invoices for the oil portrait and the word portrait, and together they would present the bills to Stuart Hammer. In person.

"I am sure," Nell said, "that it will be more difficult for him to confront the demands of two people than to play bully against just one of us alone."

"And we need to see him in person," Ann said insistently. "Deliver the bills right into his hands so he can't blame the post office or a pilfering neighbor and claim he never got them."

"We'll bolster each other up," Nell said stoutly. "Defend each other. We'll bully *him!*"

Ann had pictured them bursting in on Stuart in his office at Talcott, but Nell argued for bearding him in the Has-Bean mansion. In the end, Ann's curiosity won the day.

"I'd love the see the place," she confessed. "I'd love to see the photograph of old Minnie Poole."

And so, on a Saturday afternoon when they were pretty sure Stuart Hammer would be home and they hoped that Ramona O'Hara would not be, Nell and Ann drove to Ipswich and headed down the long drive to the mansion.

"It's more of a road than a driveway, isn't it?" Ann observed as they made their way down the long, sycamore-lined drive.

"I've clocked it," Nell said. "It's a quarter of a mile."

Ann gave a low whistle. "I'd hate to plow it in a snowstorm."

"I doubt that's a problem," Nell told her. "I'm sure Stuart calls up some plow guy and pays him off in Minnie Poole's shekels."

"Holy cow," said Ann as the drive ended in a circular turn-around and the Has-Bean mansion stood revealed in all its brick and stone, stuccoed and timbered glory.

"Ghastly, isn't it?" Nell remarked, switching off the ignition.

She and Ann stood at the front door and pressed the bell. Twice, then a third time. They could hear the bell ringing inside. The women turned to look at each in some dismay. They hadn't counted on Stuart not being home, not answering the bell.

"Plan B?" Ann asked.

But as they were starting to turn away, the heavy door was drawn in abruptly, revealing Stuart Hammer in shirtsleeves and looking very surprised to see them.

"Yes," he brought out finally, "how can I help you ladies?"

"Well, perhaps you could ask us in for starters," Nell said crisply.

She recovered her aplomb much more quickly than Stuart, who, unable to think what to say next, finally pulled the door slightly more open and stepped aside in a reluctant gesture of admittance.

Once in the foyer, Nell got right to the point. She was aware that Ann's attention had been diverted however, and that she was looking around her. Goggling was more like it. Nell gave her friend a sharp nudge.

"We're here on business, Stuart, "Nell said briskly. "This isn't a social call."

Ann, who had regained her focus, backed Nell up with a brisk nod of validation. Stuart Hammer remained mute. He put one hand on the foyer table as if for support.

"We," Nell nodded toward Ann, "have both accepted work from you, Stuart. In Ann's case, a commission to paint a very large oil portrait of your wife Ramona O'Hara, and in my case, a contract to write a sort of autobiography—what you called a 'word portrait' of Ramona. We have both completed our tasks and fulfilled our contracts to the levels described, and we are here to deliver final invoices for our work and to collect from you our final compensations. When we have those checks in hand, Ann will deliver the portrait and I will sign off on the autobiography and see that the copyright is registered to you."

Nell opened her bag and removed a white business envelope. Ann did the same. Simultaneously, they presented them to Stuart Hammer.

He made no move to accept the envelopes. He simply continued to stand beside the round table with his arms limply at his side. Nell made a small thrusting motion with her envelope but Stuart ignored it. Finally, Nell and Ann stepped forward and placed their envelopes side by side on the table.

"My terms are two-ten-net-thirty," Nell told him. "I expect Ann's terms are similar."

Without a word, Stuart stepped to the door, jerked it open and ushered the women through it.

"I don't think he spoke six words the whole time," Ann said when the carved oak door had slammed behind them and she and Nell were standing outside the Has-Bean mansion in the thin winter sunshine.

"That slammed door certainly said something though." Nell looked back over her shoulder.

"Let's get out of here." Ann shivered. "By the way, suppose he ignores our terms. What then?"

"Well, he *will* ignore them," Nell told her friend. "That's exactly what any self-respecting passive aggressive individual would do, isn't it? But to answer your question what then, I dunno know. There's always legal recourse, I suppose."

"He'd argue we hadn't performed as agreed upon," Ann said bitterly. "He'd say the painting didn't look like Ramona and some lawyer would back him up. And as for the word portrait, he'd point to you and cry: Liar! Liar!"

Unhappily Nell dug her car keys out of her bag. Ann was right. She knew that.

"Well, we've done the best we can for now," she said consolingly. "Let's just wait and see."

Chapter 33

WDDT, the North Shore's local TV station, featured an investigative team called *Spy Eye* that was charged with either cleaning up the North Shore or muck-raking about in it, depending on your view of *Spy Eye's* activity *du jour*. *Spy Eye* was a team of exactly one; a youngish woman named Hilary Justus was the whole team. Also, if truth be known, WDDT's spying eye was a little bit cross-eyed. Just enough to distract Nell from whatever news Hilary Justus was reporting and enough to cause her instead to wonder which of Hilary's eyes was off kilter. They seemed to switch roles—one time the right one wandered, the next night it seemed to be the left. Estropia, this condition was called. Nell looked it up finally in an effort to actually listen to Hilary Justus's reporting instead of examining her eyes. Being able to name the condition helped, but not much.

The spying eye was presently conducting an expose on prostitution on the North Shore, a series that Nell had been following with minimal interest. Every evening for the past week, Hilary Justus had revealed another example of small-time prostitution going on in massage parlors and fitness studios and one rather memorable set-up in a bakery well known for its gourmet cupcakes. Bunty Whitney, however, was following this feature avidly, and since Bunty had invited Nell over for a pick-up supper, the television set was droning away.

"Wait! Hold that thought a second!" Bunty commanded, waving her hand to shush the point Nell was making. "I want to see this."

And Nell had no choice but to shush and turn her attention to the set where the screen was filled with Hilary Justus, looking very serious.

"Tonight," Hilary Justus informed them solemnly (Nell observed that tonight the left eye was turning inward), "*Spy Eye* is focusing on a North Shore madam who manages a small string of 'recreational ladies'. Although the 'practitioners' are scattered all around the North Shore in a number of locations, the ring's operational base is in a Beverly massage parlor called Tenderly.

Nell sat up with a jerk.

Hilary Justus was proud to announce that *Spy Eye*'s spying eye had led to the madam's arrest.

"She is the wife of a prominent professor at Talcott College," Hilary Justus confided to her audience. "Ramona O'Hara is the wife of Dr. Stuart Hammer, the college's professor of western civilization—a well-known authority on the Etruscans."

"Oh! My! Goodness!" Nell rose to her feel in slow disbelief.

"What?" Bunty asked, "Didn't you know he was an authority on the Etruscans?"

Nell sat back down. Bunty told her that her mouth was open. Nell closed it. Her eyes, however were riveted on the television screen and she caught a glimpse of Ramona O'Hara being escorted from an automobile and hustled into a building.

"Ms. O'Hara was arrested this afternoon and taken to Salem District Court," said Hilary Justus in a voice-over as the hustling scene was taking place, "where she will be arraigned on charges of solicitation. Ms. O'Hara allegedly managed a small ring of suburban woman who range in ages from twenty-nine to forty-seven and all of whom are married. Ms. O'Hara allegedly matched up these women with men who approached her seeking services. Ms. O'Hara admitted to the charges and even described herself as the business manager of a freelance prostitution operation."

"You really know how to pick 'em," Bunty said to Nell. "Who are you getting for your next client? An axe murderer?"

But Nell was numb. She had listened sympathetically to Ramona O'Hara's story and the woman had never once admitted, even alluded to, her sideline business. And she, Nell, had never dreamed that Tenderly—the little storefront business that Ramona was so bravely starting up in Beverly—could simply be a front for prostitution. Business manager of a freelance prostitution operation, indeed! Moreover, she, Nell, had been an accomplice! She had designed and written the trifold brochure that described the benefits of Tenderly as well as the expertise of the therapists. Expertise! Nell was horrified.

The next morning, earlier than Nell was accustomed to receiving phone calls, Ann Fitzmaurice was on the line. Franklin had seen the newscast.

"Franklin actually watches WDDT," Ann said in some disbelief. "I didn't think anyone else did. Can you believe this, Nell? What do you suppose will happen?"

But Nell was at a loss for an answer.

Chapter 34

As it happened, *Spy Eye* and Hilary Justus were able to accomplish what Nell Bane could not. While Stuart Hammer could blandly overlook the facts Ramona O'Hara had tried to establish in the memoir Nell had written—and while he could insist that Nell had simply written fiction, a pack of lies—he could not escape hearing the allegations of Hilary Justus, *Spy Eye*, WDDT and the Essex County court system. The facts were public. So was the scandal. And after two days, the shame washed up the lawns of Talcott College and stopped at the Administration Building where the president was huddled in her office with the dean of the history department and the school's human resources director. They discussed the Stuart Hammer issue.

Nell could imagine the scene.

It was impossible for this trio to ignore the situation. For one thing, the WDDT van was parked right outside the administration building, and Hilary Justus was waiting to pounce on any one of the three of them as soon as they emerged from the building. Since they were not eager to emerge, Hilary Justus was spending her time pacing on the sidewalk with microphone and camera at the ready, hoping to waylay a passing student or two and score a tasty sound bite. The decisions makers couldn't afford to delay.

The dean cited Stuart's long teaching record with the college.

"He may be an odd duck," the dean conceded, "but he is a tenured professor."

The woman from HR observed that certain clauses in the school's by-laws referred to moral turpitude as grounds for dismissal—clauses powerful enough to even trump tenure.

The dean, with an edge in his voice, countered that it wasn't Stuart Hammer who was accused of moral turpitude, it was his wife.

HR answered with a sniff that seemed to imply guilt by association.

The president wondered if Hammer, faced with dismissal, might hire an attorney and bring suit against the school.

HR made a sour face as she mulled over this possibility. The dean massaged his chin. The president tapped her pen on her blotter the way a drummer would tap out a paradiddle. A gloomy communal silence settled upon the room like smog.

The human resources director rose from her chair and paced up and down the president's office in an unconscious parallel to Hilary Justus's pacing on the sidewalk outside.

The president floated the possibility that a leave of absence could get Stuart Hammer out of the way until "this whole smelly thing" blew over.

"Well, we'd better do something," HR warned, stopping at the window, "and we'd better do it fast."

Three faces, pressed to the window, looked down on Hilary Justus who had found young Jeffrey Gomblatt and was shoving her microphone into his face. Gomblatt, who was churning noisily through Talcott with an eye toward Suffolk Law School, was leaning eagerly toward the microphone and gesturing expansively.

The president made a decision. She would call Stuart into her office—call him on the carpet, so to speak—and give—no, *order*—him to take a leave of absence for six months. That should give him time to recover from whatever emotional anguish he was enduring as well as give him time to— literally—get his house in order. It should also be enough time for "this whole smelly thing" to diffuse.

The dean and the HR woman nodded reluctantly. And with their agreement, the president of Talcott College made arrangements to invite Stuart Hammer to a meeting.

Chapter 35

Nell was having her own difficulty absorbing the current events swirling around Ramona O'Hara who was standing in the maelstrom's public eye. Nell had never known—and Ramona had certainly never hinted—at another, hidden side to her life. Why had Ramona never revealed—nor Nell suspected—these extra-curricular activities? Nell was having trouble inserting these new facts into the fabric of the life she'd so carefully chronicled. She felt duped. Disillusioned. How long had Ramona been running this prostitution ring she wondered? How did she start? And why? How did she acquire her...what?...staff? And her clients...where did she find them? And was this endeavor lucrative?

"Probably more lucrative than ghostwriting," Nell muttered caustically.

And as she speculated, curiosity gnawed relentlessly at Nell Bane.

Meanwhile, her mailbox—and Ann's—failed to reveal envelopes with checks from Stuart Hammer.

"Of course with all this hoopla over Ramona's arrest and all the media attention, paying his bills is probably the last thing he's thinking of," Ann offered sensibly as she and Nell spoke on the phone.

"That's not all he has to think about," Nell told her friend. "I heard that Stuart's been given a leave of absence from teaching. Given—or ordered—to accept one. Anyhow, he's not on the Talcott campus and won't be for a while. I spoke to a young woman, a student I met when I was starting to interview Stuart, and she told me. It's hot gossip on the campus."

A calendar page was turned.

In the darkest corner of Ann's studio, the portrait of Ramona O'Hara leaned against the wall like a shamed child in time-out. A new portrait was in progress on the easel. Ann Fitzmaurice was working on a new commission—a portrait of someone's daughter who was being painted in her dressage outfit complete with helmet.

Nell was not so fortunate as to have another job under steam, and her computer screen was dark like a blind Cyclopian eye. She avoided looking at it and made soup instead—a gallon of beef stock which she planned to stash in the freezer as the base for several future soups. And as she browned the sirloin and later stirred the soup stock, she wondered and thought.

GOOD, RICH BEEF STOCK
3-4 quarts of homemade vegetable stock (see below)
1 quart of purchased organic beef or veal stock
3-4 pounds of sirloin tips cut into bite-sized pieces
Nell made the vegetable stock by selecting an assortment of vegetables from her larder: onions, several fat carrots, a shallot or two, a bulb of fennel. A small purple turnip that she'd ear-marked for a hot-sour soup was diverted instead to the vegetable stock. She slapped a couple ribs of celery on the

counter and added a whoosh of parsley. Nell spent a moment regretting the lack of parsnip, then remembered happily that she had a single sweet potato and a small butternut squash. Finally she raided the freezer for the stash of vegetable ends that she saved there. She peeled and coarsely chopped her vegetables, gave them a film of olive oil, arranged them in a roasting pan and set them to brown in a 450-degree oven, turning them as needed. When they were browned, she put them in a stockpot, added enough water to cover and simmered them for several hours. Finally she set this vegetable stock to chill.

The next day, Nell dredged the vegetables out of the stockpot, discarded them and set the liquid to boiling to reduce the stock to the desired 3 to 4 quarts.

Meanwhile, she browned the sirloin, a few pieces at a time, in a large skillet that she'd filmed with small amounts of vegetable oil. She added the browned beef and their drippings from the skillet to the stockpot, then brought the stock just to the boil and simmered it—barely bubbling—for two hours.

Nell chilled the stock overnight to let the flavors marry.

When she was ready to make a hearty soup, she could cook fresh vegetables in a small pot and add them to the stock. Then she could enjoy as much—or as little—beef vegetable soup as she wanted.

Chapter 36

"Ramona," Nell said, "I'm going to be blunt. And I hope I'm not sticking my nose too far into private space, but I am very curious to know how you went about setting up your...ah...business."

"Curious, are you?" Ramona had the kittenish smile again.

"Yes, frankly, I am."

Ramona relented. She looked remarkably calm, Nell thought, for someone who was out on bail and possibly facing a sentence.

"Okay. Well if you think back to the true confessions of my teen years in Southie—which you wrote about—you'll remember that I wasn't exactly virginal. I learned that I possessed a commodity that was negotiable. In other words, I could barter...ah...favors for things I wanted. Unfortunately the thing I thought I most wanted at the time was what was known in my family as The Drink. I was headed straight down the path Mary Claire had blazed."

Two parallel lines suddenly appeared between Ramona's

eyebrows. Nell, watching, thought she saw her friend return to those days in Southie. She waited.

"You'll also remember that I had an early apprenticeship in the backrooms of Horgan's and the Elevens. Before I was old enough to drive a car I'd learned how to handle the customers—the pleasant ones, the lonely ones, the drunks and the letches. Most of the customers were pleasant, though, but a lot of the guys who came to sit at a bar were lonely. Looking for a bit of female company. I started keeping a little black book. Over time I built quite a list."

Nell nodded. This made sense.

"But the women you hired—how on earth did you recruit *them?*"

Ramona smiled at Nell. A little sadly, Nell thought.

"You really are an innocent, sweetie."

Nell felt slightly condescended to, but she gave a small shrug.

"We aren't much different from men, you know," Ramona continued. "Some of us aren't anyway. Some of my employees were simply bored. Looking for adventure and a little danger. You know, Nell, there is something about living on the edge. Keeping a secret that would have terrible repercussions if it were known. All marriages aren't Darby and Joan, and some women did it to hurt husbands who were unkind. Like, 'ha-ha, if you only knew, you bastard'. And for others, the trade was a way to earn money. An important way—a way to put food on the table."

Ramona aimed a grave look at Nell.

"One of my gals had a husband on disability. He hadn't worked in four years. And she had three kids in school. She used the money she made for school athletic fees for the boys. And shoes. Seems someone was always outgrowing his sneakers. Sneakers aren't cheap and she begant turning tricks to buy her kids' shoes!"

Nell couldn't imagine.

"Extra money was the most common reason for getting into the business. They could make good money for a few hours work each week, and it wasn't reportable. There's no place on the tax forms to fill in prostitution."

Nell thought she was beginning to see.

"You can almost say you were running a charitable program, Ramona."

"I should have applied for 501(3) status." There was irony in Ramona's voice. "But no kidding," she looked grave. "I think all the time about Gina. How's she going to buy those sneakers now? How is Betty going to stand living with that sour old prune of a husband now?"

Chapter 37

Ramona O'Hara was free on bail, but a court date dangled above her neck like an executioner's sword. The court date was way down the corridor of time though. Nell considered that it would be full spring before Ramona would be summoned to Salem to appear before a judge in Essex County Court. Nell thought of calling Ramona, then decided not to risk it. Stuart, presumably, was spending most of his time inside the Has-Bean mansion now, having been banished from the campus of Talcott College.

Hilary Justus's spying eye had shifted to another semi-professional North Shore madam who was running a sleazy prostitution ring in one of the ramshackle houses in Salisbury Beach, now boarded up for the winter. But the story was so small-time and tawdry that even Bunty was bored.

"Enough already!" Bunty exclaimed in disgust. "It's high time Hilary moves her muck-raking into another venue."

It was the nighttime anchor of WDDT, not Hilary Justus, who importantly broke the news that sent Bunty scampering through the fence and over the frozen lawn to Nell's back door, pounding for admittance.

"He tried to kill her!" Bunty announced, pushing into the kitchen.

"What? Who? Who tried to kill whom?"

Bunty, in exasperation, explained.

"Stuart! Your friend Stuart Hammer. I just heard he tried to kill his wife!"

"Ramona?" Nell could not properly take this in. "He tried to kill Ramona? How do you know? And he's not my friend!"

"Client, then," Bunty snapped. She took a deep breath and organized her thoughts. "Okay. I was just sitting there, right? Sitting in the wing chair, having a nightcap and waiting for the late news wrap-up..."

"On DDT?" Nell asked, not bothering to keep the scorn from her voice.

"*Yes*, on DDT," Bunty snapped. "If you must know, I like it. Local news. Let's me know what's going on around here and not down in Boston or Arlington or someplace all hoity-toidy..."

"Okay, okay," Nell said hastily, "I'm sorry. Go on."

Bunty exhaled loudly.

"Enough to make me forget why I raced all the way..."

"Go *on*!"

"There was an accident," Bunty summarized. "On Hammer's property apparently. An auto accident. Something about hitting a tree and Hammer's wife being rushed to the hospital."

"Hospital? Which one?"

"I'm not sure. Beverly... no I think the guy said Anna Jacques."

"Stuart?" Nell demanded. "Stuart, was he hurt?"

"I'm not sure. I didn't catch it if they said. But they did say that he whammed the passenger's side of the car into a tree. Hard. They said he was traveling at a high rate of speed."

Nell was pacing. Bunty, calm now, watched her.

"What are you going to do?"

"Right now?" Nell replied. "Nothing, but in the morning I intend to find out more. A lot more."

Bunty nodded grimly. "Good," she said, starting for the back door. Then she turned, adding unnecessarily, "If you watched the *local* news, you'd know these things too."

Chapter 38

All the energy drained out of the house in Bunty Whitney's wake. Nell, standing in the kitchen in her nightgown and robe, felt numb. The news-bite Bunty had delivered about the accident was far too brief to satisfy Nell Bane. The corner of a rug covering who-knew-how-many secrets, had been lifted, giving Nell a peek and no more. All the muscles in her neck and back were tense, and she knew sleep would be impossible.

She hurriedly turned on the television and tried to remember which off-brand channel belonged to WDDT. She found it finally, way up the channel list, but the news hour had just ended and the station was preparing to re-broadcast a selectman's meeting that had taken place the week before. Nell watched Jonathan Seymour, the First Selectman, officiously take his place in the center of the table and place before him a sheaf of papers. Nell had already heard the results of this meeting—some to-doo about a homeowner who had breached zoning laws and filled in some wetlands. This homeowner was not from Newburyport—in other words, had lived in town less than thirty years. Probably hadn't yet learned the mores and folkways of the community. Well, he'd find out soon enough.

Nell clicked through the channels just on the chance another station had caught the Hammer story. She hoped for a slow news night on one of the Boston stations but either the night wasn't slow enough or word of the accident hadn't drifted far enough south.

Her feet were freezing, and Nell realized they were bare; in her haste to answer Bunty's pounding on the door, she had dashed from the bedroom without her slippers. She tucked herself into the corner of the sofa, pulled her legs up under her, sat on her feet and tried to think.

Stuart Hammer, that mild and smiling little man—almost prissy, he was—was an enigma. He'd be the last candidate you'd nominate as a man who'd try to kill his wife. She wondered what Minnie Poole had done to inflame Stuart enough to push her down the stairs. If, indeed, he had pushed her. There was no proof of that, of course—there was only Stuart's tearful claim that his wife had suffered a terrible fall.

Apparently, Nell thought, considering, if he were stirred enough to anger—if he became infuriated enough—Stuart Hammer could be moved to inflict physical harm, perhaps even homicide.

And one could argue that Ramona O'Hara had given him enough reason. By secretly operating a prostitution ring and being exposed as a madam, Stuart Hammer's position—both his social position and his tenured position on the Talcott College faculty—were harmed. He had been forced to take a six-month leave-of-absence, and he had been humiliated.

Well, Nell didn't blame him for being angry, but still, that didn't justify...

She thought back to the incident on the stairs outside the Talcott history department. That shove had meant business.

Only her quick reflexes and a good, strong grip had saved her from pitching down those steep stairs. Granite, she remembered, and each step edged with some kind of cross-hatched steel designed to provide safer footing. But what if she hadn't caught herself on the railing? What if she had pitched forward and kept tumbling? She might not have been killed but she certainly would have been injured. And what had she done to inflame Stuart? She had simply written a truth that he didn't want to accept. So it didn't take much. And he seemed so contrite afterwards. Nell wondered who else might have ignited Stuart Hammer to murder. Were there any other skeletons in his closet?

Below her in the cellar, the ancient oil burner shifted itself into action. The house had grown cold and Nell shivered. She untangled her legs and put her freezing feet on the cold floor.

"And so to bed," she said, hoping sleep wouldn't be far off.

Chapter 39

The next morning, as soon as Nell felt it was a decent hour to do so, she looked up the number for Anna Jacques Hospital in the Newburyport phone book.

Yes, Ramona O'Hara was a patient.

Her condition? It had been upgraded to fair.

Visiting hours were 2PM to 7.

Bunty, who had checked in to see what Nell was going to do, wanted to know if she planned to visit. When she learned that Nell intended to do just that, Bunty smiled happily.

"Bunty," Nell told her neighbor, with some asperity, "you are a voyeuristic snoop."

Bunty's smile widened.

"Absolutely true," she affirmed, "but I am not a hypocrite who tries to cover it up. And I am unapologetic. Call me when you get back."

At the door to Room 413, Nell paused. Hospitals, truth to tell, made her nervous. You never knew what you were going to see. Or smell. Or interrupt. She peeked tentatively into the room. The bed nearest the door was empty—the sheet pulled taut and ready for the next patient. Thank goodness! Beyond the half-pulled curtain that screened the other bed Nell could see foot-shaped humps in the second bed, the one nearest the window. The feet of Ramona O'Hara, she assumed. She took a brave breath and tiptoed into the room. She peered around the half-drawn curtain.

Ramona was conscious, and sensing someone's presence perhaps, turned her head on the pillow to regard Nell through eyes that looked half-dazed. IV apparatus beside the bed dripped something into Ramona's arm.

"Ramona," Nell whispered, "when I heard the news of the accident, I just had to come and see you. See if you're alright."

Ramona's eyes closed for a long moment, then she opened them slowly. Her voice was surprisingly strong.

"Yeah. Basically. Apparently I have a broken shoulder— my right one—and the arm is messed up too. General cuts and bruises but they're keeping me here because of concussion. They keep running these tests—cognitive tests—and they won't really let me sleep."

This last statement was delivered with weary irritation.

Nell slid into the visitor's chair beside Ramona's bed. She leaned in now, and covered Ramona's non-IV hand comfortingly.

"I'm so sorry," she murmured. "Can you tell me what happened?"

Ramona seemed to brighten and become more energetic. It was almost like she was emerging from a fog.

"We were coming home," she said. "Coming home from a dinner out. I'd insisted we go out because we'd done nothing but blunder around and around that house for days, bumping into each other at every turn. Stuart was home all the time because the college made him take a leave of absence. Did you know that?"

Nell nodded.

"Yes, I heard about it in a round-about way. Go on."

"Well, Stuart didn't want to go out really. He'd scarcely said nine words to me all week. I knew he was angry, but I figured if we went out and sat together over a meal, some of the kinks might work out. So we went to Ithaki. My idea. I mean, who could be gloomy over Greek food?"

Ramona paused, apparently thinking.

"I guess Stuart could," she said, answering her own question. "Anyhow we ate dinner. He hardly said anything. I'd try, every now and then, to open some inane topic, but it was like talking to a wall, so I finally just gave up and concentrated on my mousakas. It was really good," she added parenthetically.

"So Stuart paid the bill, we got in the car, and he drove us home. Then, as we turned into the driveway, Stuart started pressing on the accelerator—pressing hard. I mean he started going really fast. It scared me. 'Stuart! Slow down!' I said but he wouldn't. He pressed down all the harder."

Ramona's glazed eyes, Nell saw, had drifted out of focus as she reeled back her memory, and Nell knew Ramona was back in that driveway. She held her silence, waiting. After a few moments, Ramona picked up her thread.

"Now this next part I remember very clearly. It was like everything was happening in slow motion. The headlights picked up this huge sycamore beside the driveway. The tree trunk suddenly lit up like a huge lightening flash—illuminated by the headlamps—and things went into slow motion. I could almost count the bald patches in the bark, and I realized that Stuart was aiming right for that tree! I think I screamed. Stuart jerked the wheel to the left just before we hit, so it was the right side of the car that took the blow of the crash. I mean it wasn't a direct, head-on hit. It was a sideways glancing blow. And then...then I don't remember anything."

In the silence that followed, Nell said nothing. She just sat and stroked Ramona's hand. Ramona lay against the pillow, her dark hair spread on the white hospital linen reminded Nell of a negative. Ramona's eyes opened slowly again and she gazed at Nell.

"Have you seen Stuart?" Nell asked quietly. "Was he hurt? Has he been in to see you?"

"Oh yes." Ramona's smile was ironic. "Oh, my yes. He was in here weeping like a drain. He was so-so sorry. Oh, how could such a dreadful thing have happened? He'd cooked up this tale about an animal—a raccoon in the driveway—and he'd swerved to miss it. If only that tree hadn't been in the way...and so forth and so on. On and on he went. Lashing himself verbally. Apologizing. I hadn't heard him talk that much in weeks."

Nell, nodding, thought of Bunty. Ramona was describing just the sort of behavior consistent with a passive aggressive personality.

"Was he hurt when the car hit the tree?"

"He claims so." Ramona's eyes closed again. "He came in this morning wearing one of those big white neck things..."

"Cervical collars," Nell supplied helpfully.

"Yeah, one of those, and he had his right arm in a sling. I don't think there was really anything the matter though. I suspect it was stage craft."

The two women fell silent again. Finally Nell looked at Ramona closely to see if she'd fallen asleep. She hadn't, for suddenly her eyes opened quickly.

"Oh yeah, I forgot. An Ipswich cop was in here too. Right after Stuart left. He was one of the cops who came to the accident and he wanted to get my version of the story. He wanted to know if I'd seen the animal Stuart was trying not to hit. There was no animal, I told him. I was very clear about that."

She gave Nell a direct stare, eyes wide.

"By this time I'd figured things out. Stuart hit that tree deliberately. He aimed for it. He was trying to kill me or at least maim me. See, he couldn't hit the tree head-on or he'd be in danger of risking his own selfish hide. So he drove toward it, then swerved at the very last instant. Not to avoid an animal but to get the maximum impact on the passenger side without endangering his own worthless neck."

A slow flush was seeping up Ramona's neck from under her hospital gown near her collarbone, and Nell grew alarmed. She patted Ramona's hand to try to calm her. But Ramona appeared to be fitting remembered pieces together, and she was working herself up.

"He told me a couple of interesting things, that cop. He said that Stuart was horribly distraught at the scene. Hysterical even. He kept wringing his hands and crying that it wasn't his fault, wasn't his fault. He refused medical attention though. Wouldn't go to the hospital in the ambulance. Claimed he needed to stay at the house to answer questions and see to the car and so forth. The cops and the EMTs checked him over apparently and decided he wasn't hurt. Just a little shaken up. That cervical collar...that sling...they weren't real. They were all for show!"

Nell's mind was clicking like a computer. How long would Ramona stay in the hospital? Where would she go when she was released? She certainly couldn't return to the Has-Bean mansion where Stuart Hammer might finish off the job he'd begun. Nell's writer's vivid mind began writing scenes. They'd find Ramona O'Hara dead in her bed or fallen in a heap in a hall. Stuart would claim she'd over-dosed on prescribed medicines. Or perhaps, in her present state—drugged and confused from prescription painkillers—she'd tumbled down the stairs, repeating the sad fate of her predecessor Minnie Poole.

Nell came back to reality with a jolt.

"When will you be released, Ramona? Has your doctor said?"

"He wasn't terribly specific. I know I'll be here until tomorrow at least and then he said we'd see."

"You can't go back to Stuart," Nell said fiercely. "We'll make arrangements. I'll come back tomorrow and we'll talk more. In the meantime," Nell patted the hand rapidly, "you just rest. You've got to rest."

And Nell, as Ramona obediently closed her eyes, tiptoed out.

Chapter 40

Nell made telephone calls that very morning. First to Ann Fitzmaurice to deliver a current events report. Ann hadn't known about the accident and was shocked and then suitably scandalized when she heard Nell's version of Ramona's account from her hospital bed.

"He what? The pig! Stuart looks like such a Caspar Milquetoast I can hardly believe he is capable of such violence."

"I can," Nell told her. "That shove on the stairs made me a believer."

"Are you seeing her tomorrow?" Ann wanted to know. "If you are, may I come too?"

Nell agreed to meet Ann as soon as she'd called Ramona in the morning to find out what the doctor had said and to ask when they might conveniently visit.

The call to Bunty came next, and she was as avid for details as Ann had been. But after Nell's report, Bunty grew thoughtful, even clinical. Nell heard the potter fade as the psychotherapist emerged.

"Passive-aggressives typically practice covert abuse," Bunty mused. "They generally veil their actions. Frame them in ways that make the abuse difficult to discern. In some ways, though, this makes sense. Stuart's overt aggression seems to come in short, infrequent bursts then quickly recede as he tries to cover up before the intent can be identified."

"Like?" Nell asked.

"Well, for example," Bunty said pragmatically, "he shoved you on the stairs and claimed he slipped. He even apologized. You couldn't prove the aggression. Couldn't call him on it. And after a while the victim can even begin to believe the incident never happened. The victim can even come to believe she was the one at fault."

"Huh," said Nell.

"With this event," Bunty continued, "Stuart claims to have hit the tree while trying *not* to hit an innocent little woodland animal. He was being noble, you see. Then he shows up at his wife's bedside weeping and gnashing his teeth. He's so, so sorry. Oh dear, oh dear, oh dear."

Nell, ringing off, thought she did see.

"He's dangerous though, Bunty," was Nell's parting remark.

"Oh to be sure," Bunty agreed. "Be careful!"

Finally, Nell called her old friend Robert Hutchins, with whom she hadn't spoken in a while. They had a lot of catching up to do. Living, as he did in Boston, Robert knew nothing of WDDT on the North Shore so he was surprised to hear of Ramona O'Hara's little prostitution sideline. He was interested to know that the scandal had forced Stuart Hammer out of Talcott College, at least for a while.

"The college has given out the news that he's on sabbatical," Nell reported before going to tell Robert about the auto accident on the driveway of the Has-Bean mansion.

"Whew!" said Robert when Nell finally wound up her report. "Is there anything more?"

"Not at the moment, thankfully," Nell said. "We went along so quietly, Ann and I. So innocently. Simply trying to complete our jobs and then waiting humbly to be paid for our work. Then everything hit the fan—shock, scandal, and now a murder attempt."

"*Alleged* murder attempt," Robert Hutchins corrected. "Do you think Ramona will pursue that? Get legal counsel and try to press charges?"

But Nell had no idea and was eager, finally, to change the subject.

"How are you though?" she wanted to know. "How's Jerry and how is his project progressing?"

Robert Hutchins chuckled.

"In the final throes, I gather, and heading for the finish line. He and Mrs. Senator are thick as thieves. On the phone with each other at all hours. Trawling through antique stores all over Boston and the North Shore. The senator and his wife are planning to throw a huge open house when they finally move in."

"What you've been calling The Big Reveal," Nell said.

"Right. Jerry is over the moon. I only worry that he will come down with a thud after this is all over, and he'll have some version of postpartum depression."

"Well, I'd love to see the house when it's done," Nell said. "I don't suppose there's any chance of it though. I don't move in senatorial circles."

"You could always contribute to the senator's war chest," Robert suggested evilly.

"Paying my taxes is about all I can handle," Nell said. "But listen, Robert, I'll keep you posted on the Ramona O'Hara-Stuart Hammer adventure."

Chapter 41

Ann Fitzmaurice was waiting for Nell outside Anna Jacques Hospital.

"Did I keep you waiting?" Nell asked.

But Ann shook her head.

"Just got here." She shuddered. "What is there about hospitals? Even when I'm just a visitor I get anxious."

"I'm the same," Nell told her.

But now that she was an experienced visitor to Ramona O'Hara's room, Nell guided Ann through the hospital mazes with confidence. Low voices within Room 413, however, made them pause at the open door before they tip-toed in. A woman they did not know sat in the visitor's chair. She turned sharply when Nell and Ann came around the curtain.

"Nell!" Today, Ramona's voice was bright and her eyes were alert. "And Ann! Well, this is a party. Come in, come in."

The visitor turned around in her chair to look at them. Scrutinize, more accurately. She regarded them with some suspicion.

"This is my sister," Ramona made introductions, "the baby of the family—Marie Dawn. Marie, meet Nell Bane and Ann Fitzmaurice. I told you about them."

There were murmured pleased-to-meet-you's and some scuffling and furniture shifting as Ramona's tray table was moved aside and two more visitors' chairs were swiped from the other patient's side of the room.

"You look like a different woman today," Nell told Ramona. "You must be feeling better."

"Much," Ramona said, "and the doctor is promising to release me tomorrow morning."

"Speaking of which," said Nell, "what are you going to do? Do you have a place to stay? Because if you need someplace, I could..."

But no, Ramona was going home with her sister Marie Dawn who had, Marie put in, oceans of room—simply *oceans*. Nell was furnished with a vision of an underwater realm rather like the bottom of a swimming pool, but she restrained herself from asking if Marie Dawn lived by the sea.

"Are you sure?" Ann Fitzmaurice anxiously asked, "Because Franklin and I have a guestroom that's down a quiet hall where you could get plenty of rest."

But Marie Dawn—Nell wondered if she called herself Costello or Dargan or perhaps she used a married name— wasn't letting her sister out of her sight. She was almost fierce in staking her claim to Ramona.

"When she's completely well and on her feet again, she'll visit each of you," Marie said firmly.

And Ramona, smiling, shrugged with mock helplessness.

"Has Stuart been back to visit?" Nell wondered.

The Dargans exchanged a look, then laughed.

"He looked in briefly," Ramona started to explain, "Still wearing that phony cervical collar and full of worry, but Marie started chewing into him like he was an ear of corn at an August picnic. He left pretty quickly looking scared to death."

Marie Dawn managed to look grim and smug at the same time.

Nell was about to ask if Ramona planned to press charges against Stuart for his attempt on her life, but at that moment a trio of nurses piloted a gurney into Room 413. Ramona's new roommate had obviously arrived. There was much maneuvering and murmuring from the medical staff, and then a muffled yell and several groans of protest from the patient. Nell and Ann made hurried preparations to gather themselves and leave. They whispered instructions to Ramona to keep in touch and to get plenty of rest, and they exacted promises from Marie Dawn to see that she did so. Then they waited for a good moment to make their exit dash, scurried past the adjoining bed and fled.

Chapter 42

Ramona O'Hara, released from the hospital and into the care of her sister, disappeared into Framingham, a busy town west of Boston that throbbed with arteries of traffic—the Mass Turnpike and the retail-sated Routes 30 and 9.

"Off into the sunset she goes," Nell remarked to Ann Fitzmaurice. "Vanished."

"Never to be seen again?" Ann wondered.

"Oh, I think not." Nell was quick with her answer. "I have the strongest feeling that we haven't seen—or heard—the last from Ramona O'Hara. For one thing, she'll be back in this area for her court date in Salem."

Nell wasn't sure she could have made the same statement about Ramona's husband though. It had been more than sixty days since Nell and Ann had made their little field trip to the Has-Bean mansion to deliver their invoices to Stuart Hammer. In the interim, a great deal had happened. But one thing that had not happened was payment for their services. Neither Ann nor Nell had received Stuart's check. Nell was whinging about this to Robert Hutchins as they shared a lunch at the Beacon Hill Bistro.

Robert was pragmatic.

"Have you sent statements?" he wanted to know.

"I beg your pardon?"

Robert sighed.

"You are a talented writer, Nell, but I sometimes despair of your business acumen."

Nell was annoyed. Robert, seeing this, relented.

"Look, your terms are two-ten-net thirty, I believe, is that correct?"

Nell nodded.

"Okay, that means the client may deduct two percent if the bill is paid within ten days."

Nell started to give an exclamation of surprise, then forced herself to bite this back. She had never been quite clear just what that language meant. She thought it was just boilerplate that was typically added to the bottom of an invoice. However, she swallowed her surprise and nodded—she hoped sagely.

Robert was continuing. "Then if the bill isn't settled after ten days, your terms state that you expect the full payment to arrive within thirty days."

"And if it doesn't?" Nell wanted to know.

"Then your terms have been violated and you have other recourse. For instance, you can demand interest payments that will be added onto the original amount. That is, you can if you included that statement in your terms. Did you?"

Nell, miserable, shook her head.

"Well, never mind," Robert Hutchins said kindly. "Keep sending statements every thirty days. Keep prodding the guy. Keep calling his attention to the outstanding bill. Become a pest if you have to. You have the right. Then after—what? Ninety days? One-hundred-twenty if you want to wait that long—you can take legal action if you so chose."

Legal action. That had little appeal to Nell.

"Start paying a lawyer, you mean. No thanks. That's sending good money after bad."

Nell poked at her roasted beet salad. Robert, watching her, smiled sympathetically.

"Well, let's wait and see. Maybe Stuart Hammer will actually cough up the money. More surprising things have happened. I am confident something will work out."

Nell straightened her back and tried to aim a bright smile at Robert.

"Let's speak of other things, Robert. Tell me something bright. Something happy. Tell me more about Jerry and the senator's wife. Then perhaps you can walk me up and down Charles Street. A little retail therapy might help."

Then Nell had a sad thought.

"On the other hand," she said, "I can't afford many discretionary purchases. I was counting on that money from Stuart Hammer, so I guess the retail therapy will be limited to window shopping."

"And I," said Robert Hutchins grandly, "will pay the bill for lunch."

Chapter 43

Winter melted. Gradually. Nell, eager to be out in her garden, emotionally pushed every minute. Ramona O'Hara's court date arrived, was properly observed, and Ramona, decorously and respectfully, accepted her punishment and paid her fines. Outside Salem District Court, she shook hands with her attorney and thanked him for representing her. Then she used her cell phone to call Nell Bane.

Nell was delighted to hear from her, and yes, she'd love to meet for a celebratory lunch. She promised to phone Ann Fitzmaurice right away and persuade her to join them, and, remembering Ramona's fondness for Greek food, suggested they meet at Ithaki in Ipswich.

"Unless that would bring back unpleasant associations?" Nell said, suddenly conscious of Ramona's last evening there.

But no. Ramona had no such qualms.

"It is exactly where I'd like to be," she declared. "This time in triumph!"

"Put your paintbrush down!" Nell ordered when Ann

answered her phone.

And Ann, once she had heard the plan, needed no further urging.

Ramona was blooming. Both Nell and Ann agreed to that. In fact, she looked better than she had when she was doing sittings for Ann's portrait sessions. Nell was trying to figure this out. General happiness and a sense of wellbeing she guessed.

They heard all about the court appearance and rejoiced with Ramona that she was now free and clear of legal entailments.

"Except they'll keep an eye on me, I expect. I'll have to do some light community service—which will be kind of fun. I'm actually looking forward to it."

"Are you going back to Framingham?"

"Will you stay there?"

"Where will you live?"

"What will you do?"

"Will you...um...go back to your...um...former work?"

"What do you hear from Stuart?"

Ann and Nell peppered Ramona with questions. She laughed.

"Hold on! Hold it. One question at a time."

At that moment, lunch arrived at their table. Gyros for Ramona and Ann—lamb on pita with tzatziki. ("What is tzatziki?" Ann wanted to know.) And for Nell, a Greek salad and a bowl of avgolemono. Nell was in heaven. The smooth, lemony soup with grains of soft orzo swimming in the opaque broth was perfect. It had been ages since Nell had thought of avgolemono and she knew she'd have to make some soon.

"Ummm." Ramona licked lamb juices and tazatziki sauce from her fingers. "Okay. Questions. Where shall I begin?"

"At the beginning," Nell said decisively, "and don't leave

out anything."

"Right. Well, the first question, I think, was what is tazatziki sauce. Isn't that right, Ann? Pretty simple really. Salted, drained cucumbers mixed with Greek yogurt, lemon juice and a little garlic and dill. And you wanted to know if I'm going back to Framingham. Yes, but only for a little while. I had to get the legal hassles behind me before I could put my master plan in place, but now I'm ready to begin."

A master plan! Nell and Ann leaned forward avidly.

"Go on," Nell demanded.

"I'm going shopping for a condo somewhere on the North Shore," Ramona told them. "Someplace all my own and absolutely perfect."

"Uh." Nell sat back in her chair and tried to frame the next questions delicately. She was aware that Ann—probably reading her mind or else avid to know the same thing—was looking at her in an encouraging way.

Nell began again. "Um... Ramona... how... well I mean—can you—*afford* to buy a condo?"

Ramona took a large bite of gyro. A splatter of tazatziki sauce hit her plate. She chewed carefully and swallowed. Then she beamed at her two friends.

"Yes. It's as simple as that. Yes, I can afford to purchase a lovely condo, and I can furnish it just exactly as I damn well please. And I won't have to look at the turn-of-the-century tat that filled the Has-Bean mansion."

"How..." Ann began, then she turned a deep shade of rose, "I mean it's none of our business, but can you manage ...?"

Her question drifted off. Nell, watching Ramona's expression, held her breath.

"I was a good businesswoman, remember," Ramona said. "I squirreled away most of my earnings while Stuart and I were together, and while legal costs and fines took a deep chunk, there is still a fairly handsome remainder."

She paused.

"And there's something else. And this gets into one of the questions you asked about Stuart."

Ramona's eyes glittered.

"Stuart is paying me off. I told him I wanted out of the marriage. Well, it was over anyway, the marriage. After Stuart learned about my—um—career, he started making plans to boot me out of Minnie Poole's house. Get me out of the scene. And given the notoriety my extracurricular job kicked up, I seriously doubt a judge would have required him to pay alimony even if I'd asked. Lucky for me that Stuart was angry enough to try to wipe me out against that tree."

"Lucky?" Nell echoed. "You could have been killed."

"Yes, and I used that as my trump card. I went to see him and I cut a deal."

Nell's eyes widened. Ann licked her lips. They waited. Ramona O'Hara smiled a small, kittenish, secretive smile. Nell was reminded of Vivian Leigh—Scarlett O'Hara sitting on the great porch of Tara.

"I suggested—merely *suggested*—that Stuart might like to make a handsome settlement upon me. Otherwise I might start to remember that night in the driveway."

"You blackmailed him!" Nell breathed.

"I prefer to call it hush money," Ramona told her archly. "Once the money was safely in my account—in my account, mind you—I swore to Stuart that I would forget the whole nasty event. And if I couldn't remember it, I couldn't go to the police with the story, could I? On the other hand, if he didn't pay me, my memory would be needle-sharp. As sharp as my vindictiveness."

"So he paid you?"

"Not yet," Ramona said, and there was something

hardening in her eyes. "When the money is in my account...not promised...no check-is-in-the-mail thing...when I see the deposit noted on my bank statement, then and only then will amnesia set in."

Ramona had finished her gyro. She crossed her knife and fork and laid them across the plate. She looked up with a smile of satisfaction.

"Stuart Hammer," she stated, "is not a generous man. It took me quite a while to figure that out. He certainly seemed generous before we were married, but I gradually found out that he doesn't like to pay for anything. In fact, and not to put too fine a point on it, Stuart Hammer is a cheap son of a bitch."

Ann and Nell exchanged knowing looks, but Ramona continued.

"It must be galling him beyond all measure to have to give me the amount of money I am demanding. He'll do it though. He'll have to. It's his only salvation."

She leaned back in her chair and regarded them triumphantly.

Chapter 44

Nell had a new commission. A woman named Gloria Stevenson wanted a biography of her late husband Martin. Martin was not an especially interesting man—although a wealthy one—and his widow was a minor league nitwit. Yet Nell resigned herself to the task. Writing was writing and she appreciated the money. So every Thursday she'd been meeting with Gloria to listen to and record tales of the wonderful Martin and to examine the seemingly endless inventory of amateur photographs Gloria pulled out of boxes.

"It beats writing advertising copy," Nell rationalized to Bunty Whitney.

"Or listening endlessly to psychotherapy patients droning on and on about the same old stuff that they never seem to get beyond," Bunty added.

Bunty. That's what a good friend did. Supported you unconditionally when you needed it. Told you that you were right. Bucked you up whenever you were glum.

"What're you doing with all those lemons?" Bunty wanted

to know, changing the subject.

"I was about to make avgolemono," Nell told her. "I went out to lunch yesterday with Ann and Ramona O'Hara. Ithaki had it on the menu, and I had to have it. It has been ages since I made it and I want to tweak my recipe."

"Funny you should mention Ithaki," Bunty said. "I came over to see if you wanted to ride to Ipswich with me. The Turtle's Voice ordered a bunch of chowder mugs, and I'm set to deliver them."

"Sure," Nell was game. "The lemons will keep. I didn't think turtles had voices."

"Apparently this one does," Bunty said.

And so in Bunty's good company, Nell rode down Route 133, retracing the route she'd taken the day before. Bunty grumbled as she drove along Ipswich's busy High Street then waited at Market Square to turn onto South Main. Cars abruptly backed out of parking spaces, pedestrians suddenly took the notion to dart across streets. Bunty, applying the brakes sharply, flinched as the carton of chowder mugs made a rattling shift in the backseat.

"No damage!" Nell reported, rising up in her seat to crane her neck into the carton.

They spotted the sign for The Turtle's Voice just ahead, and in front of it, miraculously, was a parking space. Bunty swerved into it with a casual professionalism.

But inside the shop a problem presented. The shopkeeper was harried this morning. She'd meant to pop into the bank to get cash to pay Bunty and what with one thing and another, hadn't accomplished the errand. She started to tell Bunty and Nell in excruciating detail every single thing that had tripped her up.

Nell, growing impatient, had an idea.

"Listen, why don't you write a check to cash and I'll run

up to the bank while you and Bunty are unloading the mugs. Then I'll hurry back with the cash, you can pay Bunty and we'll be out of your way."

The shopkeeper paused to think this over. Apparently she couldn't see anything wrong with this scheme and decided to be grateful. Nell was grateful too. She thought she'd go mad if she had to stay one more moment in this shop with this demented woman. With the check onboard, she trotted up the street.

The old Downeast Savings Bank was familiar to Nell for she had an account in the Newburyport branch. This connection would make it easier to get the Turtle lady's check cashed. Nell took her place in the teller line behind a man with a hooded sweatshirt that read 'Electricity isn't a hobby. Call a professional electrician.' Nell smiled and resigned herself to wait a bit while the customer just ahead of the electrician conducted his business. He seemed to be conducting it with excruciating slowness or else was encountering difficulty because the teller had to leave her post and fetch another person—probably a manager. Both women were now attempting to sort this customer out.

Nell shifted from one foot to the other. The electrician huffed a sigh of impatience. Two more people queued behind Nell. Finally the man at the head of the line must have been satisfied, because he turned from the window. Nell frowned. She knew him from somewhere...then she gasped. It was Stuart Hammer, but she'd hardly recognized him. Hammer, busy counting bills and comparing the cash to a receipt in his other hand, didn't look up, thank goodness.

Nell couldn't believe it. He was disheveled. Unshaven. The very antithesis of the dapper little professor she knew from Ann's studio and from her own meetings with him at Talcott. He shuffled to the bank's glass doors, losing his balance slightly as he attempted to shoulder one of them open. Then Stuart Hammer blundered out into the bright daylight and turned up the street.

The electrician's business at the teller window was brief, and Nell stepped forward to cash her check. Then, with the money in hand, she hurried out of the bank, hoping to catch another glimpse of Stuart Hammer. She could hardly believe it was he. But the man had vanished.

"Well, it took you long enough," Bunty said bluntly when Nell finally bustled into The Turtle's Voice. "We're all set here. Or will be as soon as Ethel settles up."

Which Ethel promptly did, promising to be in touch with Bunty as soon as this chowder mug order sold out. Outside, Nell reported the Stuart-sighting to Bunty, who for some reason seemed terribly disappointed to miss seeing him. She looked all around, her head swiveling on her neck like a periscope on a conning tower.

"Where is he? Do you see him?"

Nell obligingly looked too, but Stuart Hammer had vanished.

"Look," said Bunty, "since we're already here in Ipswich, why not drive past the Has-Bean place so I can at least see what *it* looks like. I've been dying to see it."

But Nell demurred.

"That would be awkward, Bunty. I don't want to be seen gawking outside his property. "

"Stuff!" retorted Bunty. "He owes you money! You should have grabbed hold of him right there in the bank and marched him back to that teller window and demanded he withdraw your payment from his account right then and there."

Nell, smiling grimly, reflected that her friend was probably right. She'd missed her chance. And it would have been such a coup to report to Ann. Too late. She consoled herself that back in her kitchen in Newburyport, lemons waited.

AVGOLEMONO
Greek Lemon and Egg Soup
5 cups of chicken stock
1/3 cup long grain white rice
2 eggs
Finely grated lemon peel from 1 lemon
Juice of 1 lemon
3 T fresh parsley, chopped
Thin lemon slices

Nell brought the stock to boiling and a large saucepan. She seasoned it with salt and pepper and stirred in the rice. She covered the pot and let the stock simmer for 15 minutes, then tested the rice for tenderness.

In a small bowl she beat the eggs with the lemon peel and lemon juice. When the rice was tender, she tempered the eggs by whisking a couple of tablespoons of broth into the bowl. Then she whisked in a couple more. Finally she was ready to risk a ladleful, and when that was successfully smooth with no curdling, she whisked the egg mixture into the pan of hot stock and rice. She kept the heat low, being careful not to let the soup return to the boil, and she stirred constantly as the soup thickened and became creamy. She tasted for seasoning, and added a generous pinch of salt and a few grinds of fresh pepper. A generous sprinkle of parsley and the avgolemono was ready—ready except for the slices of lemon that Nell floated on top.

Not quite Ithaki's avgolemono but excellent nevertheless.

Chapter 45

"For heaven's sake, you two," Bunty Whitney had said. "Look at you! The pair of you! Moping around, feeling sorry for yourselves. Stand up and be women! Be proactive! Beard Stuart Hammer in his den and demand what is rightfully yours!"

And so now Nell and Ann Fitzmaurice, shamed into action by Bunty, were approaching the Has-Bean mansion once more in the hope of doing do exactly what Bunty had insisted upon—demanding payment for the work they'd done for Stuart Hammer. Nell, still under the spell of Bunty's stirring speech, felt full of purpose; full of confidence, this time she was prepared to stand up to the little goblin. Ann was more cautious. Nell gave her a pep talk.

"We have the right on our side, Ann. Stuart has breached not only the law but the ethics of our arrangements. He hasn't kept his word."

"He's ignored our statements," Ann pointed out weakly. "He ignored our invoices when we presented them so why do you think this call will have a different result?"

"We have to try!" Nell was determined. She thought briefly of the look on Bunty's face if she'd had to admit they'd weaseled out.

"Well, there's one more thing," Ann said nervously. "We could be going into the den of a murderer. He tried to wipe out Ramona, and we have reason to think he might have helped Minnie Poole into her grave. Nell, we could be in danger."

"That's why we're going in broad daylight," Nell answered patiently. "And why we're going together. We have him outnumbered and he's not a large nor formidable man."

"We're not large either," Ann murmured.

"This is our last ditch stand," Nell said grimly. "The last call."

With a firmness she did not actually feel, Nell switched off the ignition and got out of the car, banging the door unnecessarily hard behind her, perhaps as a rehearsal for the firmness she planned to show toward Stuart Hammer.

Four rings on the doorbell of the Has-Bean mansion brought no result. Ann looked helplessly at Nell, but Nell had worked herself up by this time. With Ann trailing, she marched around to the back of the house and banged noisily on the door that she knew led to the kitchen. She banged again, longer this time. Her fist hurt and she rubbed it on her thigh. But this time the curtain covering the glass moved and Stuart Hammer's startled face looked out. The curtain dropped back into place.

"Stuart! Let us in," Nell shouted. "This is your last chance before we start legal proceedings against you!"

There was silence. Perhaps Stuart was thinking this over or perhaps he was continuing to ignore them. They heard the door unlock.

"Fear got to him," Nell whispered to Ann, as the door was pulled inward.

Nell heard Ann give a small, involuntary gasp as Stuart Hammer stood revealed in his unkempt state. Half his shirttail was pulled out of his trousers. He was in bedroom slippers and his bare ankles looked cold and vulnerable. As he had been when Nell had seen him, he was unshaven. And he looked haggard.

"Well?"

"Stuart," said Nell reasonably, "may we come in? We won't stay, but we need to speak to you about your outstanding debts to us. To both of us."

By way of cold invitation, Hammer held the door wider. As they stepped inside, Nell saw that the kitchen was in a state similar to Stuart's. The handles of unwashed skillets sprouted from the sink like a weird metal bouquet, a loaf of bread, half unwrapped, was splayed on the kitchen table next to three open jars of jelly and an assortment of sticky table knives. There was a sour smell in the room and the floor felt gritty. But Stuart spoke with a dignity that was almost vaudevillian.

"I am aware of the invoices you have presented," he told them haughtily, "but I do not believe I am under any obligation to pay them. The work you did—both of you—was substandard. Not what I asked for at all. And it is not my custom nor habit to pay for inferior work."

He frowned at Ann.

"You are obviously not the professional artist you claim to be. You misrepresented yourself. You couldn't begin to capture the essence of Ramona. And you," he continued, turning to Nell, "produced nothing more than a pack of lies. Fiction and wild imaginings. I ought to have you brought up on charges of slander for what you wrote!"

He drew himself to his full height.

"That is all I have to say on these matters. Now I'll ask you to leave."

"Stuart," said Nell with some heat in her voice, "your position is legally indefensible, but it is also unethical. And I believe you know that. Have you no sense of decency?"

"All I have to say on the matter," Hammer repeated. He stepped to the door and opened it.

They were at a stand-off.

"If you don't leave immediately," he said, "I shall be forced to call the police and have your removed and charged with trespassing."

Ann and Nell exchanged looks.

"And that is your final position?" Nell said.

"It is."

With that, Nell and Ann moved past him and out of the house.

"Well, we tried," said Ann pragmatically, as the car was safely heading down the driveway.

Nell identified the sycamore that had most likely been Hammer's target—the one he must have earmarked for Ramona's demise. The trunk bore fresh scars. More of the pale skin showed, and where the bark was torn away, she could see fresh yellow wood. She closed her mind and drove past.

"Franklin suggested we might have to resign ourselves to writing off the work as bad debt," Ann continued as Nell glanced back at the tree. "He said we just might have to chalk these debts off as learning experience.

Nell, who couldn't think of anything to say to this, had to humbly agree.

Chapter 46

Nell paged idly through her collection of soup recipes, looking for an antidote to the maunderings of Gloria Stevenson and her tribute to the late Martin that she was supposed to be writing. Yes, black bean soup would do. There were a number of steps to the recipe and Nell could work at the computer, embroidering tales of marvelous onderful Martin while the beans soaked and simmered.

BLACK BEAN SOUP
1 cup black beans
1 medium onion, finely chopped
2 T vegetable oil
1 bay leaf
5 cups water
5 cups vegetable or chicken stock
1 yellow bell pepper, seeded and diced
1 garlic clove, crushed

1/3 cup brown rice

4 oz. ham, diced

Allowing herself plenty of time to prepare the black beans, Nell washed and picked the black beans, put them in a large saucepan, covered them with cold water and set the pan on the heat. When the water had boiled for 2 minutes, Nell covered the pan and took it off the heat and left the beans alone for 2 hours.

After 2 hours, Nell drained the beans and wiped the saucepan clean. Then the pan went back on the stove and Nell cooked the onions in the vegetable oil, stirring until the onions browned. She added the water, the beans and the bay leaf to the onions, brought the ingredients to boiling , then covered the pan and simmered the bean mixture for close to 2 hours.

Nell drained the bean mixture, and once again cleaned the pan. Back in went the bean mixture along with the stock, bell pepper, garlic and rice. Nell seasoned this with salt and pepper and set the pan on the heat to simmer for an hour. She checked the beans for tenderness and decided to simmer the soup for a half hour longer.

When the beans were tender, Nell added the diced ham to the soup and tasted for seasoning. She fished out the bay leaf and pronounced the soup ready.

Chapter 47

Nell turned off Eastern Avenue onto Beach—a short, bumpy, downhill bit of road, more of an over-used shortcut really— between the Ledgewood Farms condominium complex and a small shopping mall anchored by a Stop and Shop. Below them, where Beach ended at Thatcher, Nell and Ann Fitzmaurice could see the wide spread of salt marshes and the ocean beyond.

"Seems Ramona has landed herself in the high rent district," Ann said. "Impressive."

Nell was impressed too. Gloucester's Ledgewood Farms was an enviable community built on a hill with the units positioned somewhat randomly, wherever the huge outcroppings of granite had permitted foundations to be excavated. The dwellings were stained a uniform gray that perfectly matched the granite. Wide balconies and glass walls permitted each homeowner a panoramic view of marsh and ocean.

Ramona O'Hara was nothing if not surprising. Nell,

reflecting on this, smiled as she shook her head. Ramona had lost little time putting her master plan to work and from this, Nell inferred that Stuart Hammer's money had made its way into Ramona's bank account. And to celebrate her achievement and the launch of the master plan, she had invited Nell and Ann to lunch in her new condominium. Nell had marveled, when the invitation came, that Ramona had been able to achieve what she and Ann, with their invoices and statements and their badgering and threats, had not. She had spoken to Bunty about Ramona's success.

"Does this have anything to do with Stuart's passive-aggressive personality?" Nell wondered.

Bunty had considered this.

"Ramona," she said, "was able to identify Stuart's Achilles's heel. She figured out what could hurt him—what he would be afraid of—and she leveraged that fear."

Nell's confusion slowly melted into recognition.

"Ah-ha," she said softly, "so he was afraid she really would go the police and accuse him of trying to murder her."

"Sure, that," Bunty agreed, "but he probably knew her accusation would be spot-on. Knew it was true. But even if it weren't true, he would still have to defend himself in the legal venue and that would mean he'd look bad—very bad—in the eyes of the community. And it would certainly seal his fate with Talcott College. Stuart's position with the college is very important to him. It contributes enormously to his self-perception."

Nell's mental motor had hummed. How, she wondered, could she and Ann use that Achilles's heel to leverage their own payments? Or was it too late?

Nell turned onto Thatcher and almost immediately turned again and through the gates of Ledgewood Farms.

Ramona O'Hara was radiant. And eager to show her first

guests through her new home.

"Now," she said as they stood at last on the balcony exclaiming over the views, "Champagne cocktails are the order of the day. To toast new beginnings."

"I've never known quite how to make a champagne cocktail," Ann remarked.

"You forget," Ramona told her, "that I was a mixologist in a former life. Among other things."

She laughed.

Mixologist?" Ann asked, puzzled.

"Bartender to you, dear," Ramona translated kindly.

"And speaking of former lives and other things," Nell said, when she was holding a slender flute of Champagne and after toasts had been proposed. "What profession do you intend to pursue now? Do you intend to return to a former one or head for new horizons?"

Ramona was thoughtful.

"One of the reasons I wanted to be in Gloucester was for the abundance of watering holes in the town. Rockport was dry for years and years but Gloucester rocks! Always has."

She leaned her arms on the balcony railing and appeared to focus on the distant horizon, gazing up toward Twin Lights perhaps.

"Actually, I'm thinking of continuing in the hospitality business. Oh no!" she amended quickly, seeing the scandalized looks on the faces of her two friends. "Not that segment! No, no. I learned my lesson. I'm going to open a small restaurant. A bistro. It'll have a bar of course, which I will oversee, but I'll also play the host. Be the head honcho. I have a partner, an old friend, who'll head up the kitchen. It's going to be terrific."

Nell smiled.

"And what are you going to call this place?"

"Why *Ramona's*, of course!"

Instantly, champagne flutes were raised again as Nell and Ann toasted Ramona's and the new venture.

"Much success!" declared Ann stoutly. "To Ramona and to Ramona's!"

And Nell added "Hear! Hear!"

"Now you have to have a sample of Ramona's menu. Peter, my partner, sent it over specially."

And Ramona got busy in the kitchen serving up a lunch that Nell and Ann pronounced delicious.

But over coffee, Ramona had another surprise. She introduced the subject off-handedly.

"Did Stuart ever pay you for your work? Either of you?"

As Nell and Ann ruefully shook their heads, Ramona grew thoughtful.

"Well, here's the thing. I would like to buy the oil portrait, Ann—the one that Stuart commissioned and never paid for. It is far too big and ostentatious to hang in anyone's home, but it would be perfect in the bistro. It would be the centerpiece of Ramona's."

Ramona reached across the small table to cover Ann's hand with her own. Ann was staring at her with a lack of comprehension that made Nell smile.

"And Nell," Ramona continued, "I want to purchase the autobiography too. As you and I worked on it together, I learned a lot about myself. The work put my life in some kind of perspective. While it served as a mirror—allowed me to see who I was and where I'd been—it also inspired me to change directions. I've reinvented myself a couple of times. Perhaps the first was when I got clean and sober. But the second reinvention was when I escaped from Stuart Hammer and life in the Has-Bean mansion."

"I think that second reinvention was more of a rebirth, don't you?" Nell said drily. "A resurrection where you died to an old life and were regenerated. Born anew."

"Ah," Ramona said. "Perhaps so. But in any case, the autobiography, memoir, whatever you'd call it, set me in a new direction. While I was staying with my sister in Framingham, I read it over and over. Marie read it too, and we laughed together when we read about Mary Claire and how we Dargans grew up in Southie. It brought back to us so many memories— good and bad—and we laughed and laughed, but we cried a little too. So thank you for giving us back memories we might have otherwise lost."

"Are you sure you want to do this?" Nell asked. "Ann and I don't come cheap."

"Absolutely sure," Ramona said emphatically. "Make those invoices intended for Stuart over to me—and don't cut any corners. Don't give any discounts. I'll need the invoices for my records, but I am prepared to write the checks right now."

Ramona disappeared into a bedroom. Nell and Ann exchanged glances.

"Should we let her do this?" Ann whispered.

"I heard that!" Ramona said, coming back into the room whacking her checkbook against her palm. She fixed a severe gaze upon Ann, who looked properly chastened. "You'd better! You'll never get a better offer."

Heading home—Thatcher to Beach, then the difficult left turn that put them on Eastern Avenue, and finally onto Route 128 that would take them as far as 133—Nell and Ann were mostly silent. Overwhelmed by the events of their day with Ramona O'Hara, they squinted into the solar glare of late afternoon and thought their individual thoughts.

"I think the bistro—Ramona's—will be a success, don't you?" Ann said finally.

"Bound to be," Nell answered. "That woman has more grit and determination than any three people together."

A few more miles were accomplished in silence.

"Gosh, that gesture of hers—taking over bills we'd given Stuart—what an incredibly grand gesture." Nell was thinking of the check tucked comfortingly inside her handbag.

"D'you think she meant it?" Ann wondered, "All that stuff about wanting the portrait for the restaurant and all that other stuff about memories and new directions?"

Nell shrugged. "If she didn't mean it, she is a very convincing actress. But yes, I think she was sincere. I think Ramona O'Hara truly is reborn."

They started up Route 133 and were nearly in Essex. Antique shops were appearing with greater frequency, and Nell had another thought.

"It's funny isn't it? I mean the way things turn out? We got paid for our work after all."

"Yeah, thanks to Ramona," Ann said.

"Yes. Technically. But you could look it another way." Nell was thoughtful. "Ramona was the *vehicle*, but *Stuart* was the source. She used some of his money to pay us. He didn't know about it, but his money did come to us in the end because it was channeled through Ramona."

Ann started to laugh, and Nell joined her. They laughed their way up Route 133 and right into the center of Essex.

The road north of Essex veered right and Nell steered the curve.

"You know, Ann," Nell said as they drove into the pastureland that took over from coast, "that portrait of Ramona—that is really something. Stuart Hammer is an ass. You caught more than a likeness. You somehow caught her innate, illusive, inestimable beauty—the beauty she has inside."

Chapter 48

It was the night of the Big Reveal—Jerry Gasso's gala event—so long anticipated and looked forward to. Franklin and Ann Fitzmaurice had generously offered Nell and Bunty a lift to Beacon Hill where there they would join up with Robert Hutchins, and the little party would make their way on foot to Louisburg Square. For the house of the senator and his wife was finished—the last lick of paint applied to walls, the last antique mirror hung, the floors given one last whirl with a buffer. Nell envisioned elaborate flower arrangements being trotted in from Winston's, trays and crates being hefted from caterers' trucks and cartons being shunted in by deliverymen from Boston's best purveyors of liquor. The senator and his wife, whose name Nell couldn't remember—Jerry always called her Beauticia and Nell hoped she wouldn't slip up and say that when they were introduced—were hosting a huge bash to celebrate the completion of their house. Jerry, who had been deep in the dingles of the project from the start, was to be a guest of honor, and he had been encouraged to ask whomever he wished.

So now, dressed to the nines, Nell was seated next to Bunty in the upholstered backseat of Franklin's black Mercedes and heading toward a glittering, and very unaccustomed, evening. Bunty was dressed to the nines too, and Ann's best diamonds shot sparks from her ear lobe when she turned to speak to them over the seat. Nell had to envy Ann's taste and sense of style. Never overdone nor tasteless, Ann Fitzmaurice always managed to look impeccably tailored and head-turningly smart. Nell, struggling to achieve a similar effect, never felt she'd succeeded.

Bunty Whitney's sense of style was another matter. She had chosen a flowing number for the evening. It was new—or at least new to Bunty—who did her "dressed up" shopping at Newburyport's consignment shops. Bunty was a mistress of accessory though and to the gown, had added a remarkable scarf. ("Long enough to have strangled Isadora Duncan," Bunty remarked rather crudely, as she released the scarf from the car door's entrapment and dragged its tail inside. She rewound it about her neck and shoulders.) She had piled her considerable hair on top of her head, the better to show off an elaborate pair of earrings.

"Damn," said Bunty.

An earring had caught in the scarf, preventing her from turning her head. Nell helped her unhook it.

"Hold still," Nell commanded. "You're wiggling like a trout on a line. There! Got it."

"Thanks," said Bunty.

Robert Hutchins, looking very handsome, was waiting for them in the townhouse he shared with Jerry.

"Evening clothes," Nell commented with satisfaction. "Perfect. Jerry will be pleased."

"And I am pleased this evening is finally here," Robert

said. "Jerry was like an ant on a hot skillet all day. Are we all ready? Share we prepare to stroll?"

Louisburg Square always gave Nell a sense of pleasure. The miniature neighborhood held within itself a unique air of reserve. Enclosed by the rest of Beacon Hill, it had its own soul—a community within a community. The brick residences ringed an ironwork fence in whose green pocket Christopher Columbus and Aristedes the Just watched over the Square with stone-cold, sightless eyes.

Tonight, there was no doubt which house was hosting a party. People moved up and down the front steps and the great door stood wide open. Nell recalled the other time she had visited this house with Jerry Gasso. The house had been vacant then, and silent except for the hollow, ringing sounds their voices and footsteps made. Something had felt ominous. The rooms had held a chill.

The façade of the senator's house put it in lockstep with the architecture of its neighbors, but the visitor, stepping into the foyer, might be shocked by the warp-speed trip through two centuries. Glass staircases floated up from the entry to expose a view of four upper floors and light flooded these staircases. In daytime, a vast skylight drenched the house with sunshine but tonight, cleverly engineered artificial light illuminated the dramatic house and turned it into a lantern.

Jerry Gasso spotted them and leaned over the second floor railing to call.

"Robert! Up here! No, no wait, I'm coming down! I don't want you to go anywhere without me!"

And Jerry, like a salmon swimming against the current, made his way to the first floor against the tide of chatting, laughing people who were moving up.

"Ann, darling! Perfect as always!" Jerry kissed Ann Fitzmaurice on both cheeks and turned to Bunty with a laugh of joy.

"Bunty, you gorgeous broad, tremendous pleasure to see you!"

Jerry grasped Franklin Fitzmaurice's hand, then abruptly pulled him into a bear hug and thumped his shoulder.

"And Nellybean! Last but best."

Jerry, grasping both Nell's hands, held her away from himself so he could take her in. "Lovely! Lovely! And I can't wait for you to see the joint."

"The Big Reveal, eh?"

"Indubitably. Now," he cried, easily assuming the role of host, "everybody must have something to drink. Then I must introduce you to the senator and Susan. Come."

Susan. Thank goodness! Nell was relieved. Susan. That was the senator's wife's name. And almost immediately, Nell found herself in this woman's presence, and Jerry was making rapid introductions.

Evidently Susan, the senator's wife, was accustomed to meeting people in herds for she didn't appear to be daunted in the slightest. She shook hands and dimpled and made small sounds of pleasure, and when the introductions were over, asked, "Well, what do you all think of the place? We absolutely couldn't have done this without Jerry. And we've become unnaturally close, haven't we Jerry?"

She winked at him.

Jerry threw an arm around Susan's shoulders and yanked her close.

"We have indeed, Beauticia. Ah, what the senator doesn't know."

"He doesn't know how much we spent, that's for sure," the woman retorted. And this sent Jerry and Susan into an immoderate chorus of laughter.

Nell found herself smiling. She was so happy for her

friend's triumph, and she was looking forward to Jerry's tour.

Up and down they went, all of them exclaiming over spaces and objects and boggling at the stories Jerry told as he pointed out furnishings and related domestic disasters that now—at least in Jerry's telling—seemed uproariously funny.

"There was a wall there, just there, and now it's *space*. This house is narrow, you know, and we needed to create visual volume."

"Visual volume," Nell repeated to herself. "My goodness."

"The elevator pays homage to the nineteenth century while honoring the twenty-first..." Jerry was saying. His guests stood in a row trying to absorb this concept.

They goggled at abstract paintings juxtaposed with bergeres incongruously wearing animal print upholsteries instead of velvets. They gazed at a piece of four-hundred-year-old pottery from China exhibited on a pedestal of twenty-first-century Lucite.

"And can you believe," cried Jerry Gasso, "that a printed Indian sari could become such a fantastic bedspread?"

Nell, for one, could never have imagined it.

"The tour's over," Jerry announced, "I must check in with Beauticia, so you are all on your own. Mingle now, children." Jerry wiggled his fingers at them. "Mix and mingle and make new friends."

And Nell, turning, did find herself on her own. She looked down at the glass she was holding. Still half full. That was good. Less danger of spillage and enough wine left to buy immunity against any good-hearted soul eager to fetch her another drink.

Bunty Whitney had fallen into animated conversation with a man Nell did not know. They seemed to be arguing about an abstract painting, but Nell couldn't tell whether either of them admired it or hated it. She wandered over to the glass staircase and couldn't resist stopping to look down. It was an amazing scene. She placed her forearms on the banister and leaned in for a better view.

"Not thinking of leaping, I hope," said a voice at her elbow. Nell turned to an elderly man smiling gently at her.

"Just considering what an amazing transformation has occurred here. A leap would really add drama to this already dramatic occasion though, wouldn't it?" Nell smiled back. "I'm Nell Bane."

"Ned Ames," the man introduced himself with a gentlemanly inclination of his head. "May I join you at this rail?"

"Please do."

Nell moved a hospitable six inches down the banister, and Ned Ames also leaned forward on his arms and surveyed the scene.

"Transformation, you said," he said, picking up Nell's remark, "perhaps. Some would say destruction. Sorry about my negative tone. I'm an architect, you see. And I've lived on the Hill all my life—seventy-eight years—and have witnessed the deplorable gutting of so many of these lovely houses."

Nell turned to look at him.

"Change is often hard," she said sympathetically, thinking of her first view of the place with Jerry. "This place, for example, experienced a wrenching death when the wrecking ball came inside, but it's had a resurrection too. I suppose the interiors of these architectural gems need to be reordered to support life in this century."

Ned Ames grunted in grudging recognition.

"Change seems to happen faster and faster," Nell continued thoughtfully, "although maybe its just my perception. As I get older, the weeks and months whizz by and time sort of collapses. Maybe that's why change seems to happen so quickly."

"You are a wise woman," Ames said softly. "Thank you for giving me another perspective. Resurrection. Something new to think about."

"Mr. Ames!"

Ned Ames and Nell turned to find Robert Hutchins joining them.

"Robert!" Ned Ames shook Robert's hand delightedly. "A pleasure to see you, my boy. I have just met the most charming lady. May I introduce you to Nell Bane?"

"Nell and I are old friends," Robert told him. "Although not as old as you and I."

He addressed Nell's surprised look.

"Ned's family has always lived just down the street from mine, so I've known him all my life."

"But not all of mine, young man," Ned Ames said. "I understand your fellow, Jerry Gasso, is partially responsible for this amazing ...*transformation*."

He peered around Robert to wink at Nell.

"That's very true," Robert said. "However, I am here to pry this charming woman away from you Ned. Nell, the others are getting their coats and Jerry will be joining us back at the house shortly. Ned, stop in for a nightcap, by all means, and you can continue to be charmed by Nell in the intimacy of my untransformed sitting room."

As Nell and Robert started down the staircase, he slipped a hand under her elbow.

"Franklin and Ann were telling me that Ramona O'Hara has picked up the bills for the work her husband commissioned. Very good news indeed. And congratulations on ending that miserable situation on a positive note."

"Isn't life strange, Robert?" Nell asked as Robert held her coat for her. "Things aren't always what they seem. The sands are shifting constantly and we have to keep on our toes to adapt to change."

"Adapt or be miserable," Robert Hutchins observed. "We have a choice to accept change or fight it."

"I think it's generally healthier to accept," Nell said "Die to the old. That way, we can be reborn—start new."

Robert finished bundling Nell into her coat and he offered his elbow.

"Ready?" he asked as the Fitzmaurices and Bunty Whitney jostled together in the foyer. "Are we all ready to step forward into our futures?"

Chapter 49

"Do you know the definition of *chutzpah*?" Ann Fitzmaurice demanded.

"Isn't 'hello' the customary greeting when phoning a friend?" Nell began, "And yeah...it means enormous gall...brazen effrontery...insolent audacity..."

"That's the long version," Ann said tersely. "Here's the short version: Stuart Hammer."

Nell was at sea.

"I'm afraid I'm not following you."

"Then listen to this," Ann snapped. "Are you still there?" she added anxiously.

"Yes," said Nell patiently, "I'm listening."

"Okay. So I'm in the studio painting. I've got Pandora playing quiet jazz, the paint's working well, everything's nice. There's a knock on the kitchen door. I go to answer it. And who do you think is standing there?"

Nell had rarely heard Ann Fitzmaurice this exercised, but

she'd been tipped off to what this story might be about, so she ventured a hesitant guess.

"Stuart Hammer?"

"Yes!" cried Ann, forgetting she had already dropped his name. "How did you...oh, never mind. He's standing there big as life and wearing this huge smile. Like we're the best of old friends who haven't been seen each other in way too long. Like we're old pals! Like nothing has ever happened between us! I was staggered.

'Ann,' he says, 'how are you?'

'Surprised,' I say. And in he comes. I mean I didn't even invite him and he steps right in as if I had and prepares to make himself at home. And he's got this woman with him."

"What woman?" Nell asked.

"I don't know. He never really introduced her. Margaret. I think he called her Margaret."

"How did he look?" Nell interrupted.

"Oh, that was the thing!" Ann said passionately. "He looked terrific. Like the old Stuart. All duded up, combed, brushed, washed, all glossy and fluffy. He had on this light gray coat that...oh, never mind—he just looked like a different guy from that slob we saw at the mansion."

"Huh," said Nell. "Well, go on."

"It was the weirdest thing," said Ann reflectively. "Like nothing unpleasant had ever passed between us. He introduced this woman—Margaret—well, he sort of introduced her; I never caught her last name. And that was all the explanation he gave. Whether she was his wife or his girlfriend or even his sister, for goodness' sake, I never found out. And I didn't *care*!"

Ann's distress had apparently returned.

"And here's the thing, Nell—he came over because he wanted me to *paint her portrait! Margaret's* portrait! And he starts saying to her, 'Ann is the premiere portrait artist on the

North Shore' and 'nothing but the best is good enough for you, my dear' and 'I want to own an oil painting of you so I can enjoy you every moment.' I would have been nauseated if I hadn't been so mad!"

"What did you tell him?" Nell asked avidly.

"Well, I told him no! What did you think I'd tell him? 'Stuart,' I said, 'If yours were the last commission I was ever offered...if I were starving in the streets of Newburyport, I would never—*never*—accept another job from you. *You never paid me for the last one!*"

"Huh," Nell said again. But Ann wasn't quite finished.

"And the man had the effrontery to look amazed. He acted like of course he had paid me and I'd just forgotten. The temerity! The *chutzpah!* It was as if he couldn't imagine what I meant. Like all those scenes with the invoices and statements and the personal demands we made at his house had never happened."

Ann wound down as if the emotion necessary to tell the tale to Nell had drained her.

Nell could hardly imagine this.

"What do you suppose is the matter with him?" she wondered. "Do you think it's some warped, psychological thing?"

"I *can't* imagine," Ann said tiredly. "I just shoveled him out the door. Margaret too. She never said a word the whole time. I can't imagine what she thought."

"What did she look like?" Nell wanted to know. "Like, was she a knock-out? A beauty?"

"No," Ann said, "She wasn't anything unusual. She wasn't not-pretty. Just an average-looking woman. Somewhere in her late 'thirties maybe."

"Did she look like Ramona?"

"No. She looked like herself. Margaret. I couldn't tell a

thing about her."

"Huh." Nell was thinking. "He must be repeating it again."

"What?" Ann wanted to know. "Repeating what?"

"He's found a new *La Belle Dame sans merci*. Our little Stuart Hammer is once again enthrall."

"Oh heaven help us!" Ann exclaimed.

"Poor woman," Nell mused. "I hope she doesn't get hurt in this relationship. Should we warn her?"

"No," Ann said firmly. "She's on her own. She may figure him out faster than we did. Faster than Ramona did. Anyhow, I've seen the last of him."

Then Ann remembered something.

"Oh! I nearly forgot. This is mostly why I called. As Stuart was leaving he said to her—to Margaret—'Don't worry, my dear, we're going to get your story written—the story of your life.' Nell! I think he's going to call you. I called to warn you!"

Nell was making soup—beef vegetable—and she'd run out of onions, darn it. But the day was pleasant and a brisk walk would do her good. She turned off the heat and trotted up to Fowle's Market and while she was there had a nice chat with the woman behind the meat counter, then she passed the time of day with Mr. Chandler from church. They were on the diaconate committee together.

When she got home, though, the red light on the answering machine was flashing. She pressed the message button to listen.

"Good afternoon, Mrs. Bane, this is Stuart Hammer..."

Nell didn't listen to the rest of the message. She pressed the 'off' button. Then she hit 'erase'.